The Maverick's Holiday Masquerade

Caro Carson

HARLEQUIN® SPECIAL EDITION®

Special thanks and acknowledgment to Caro Carson for her contribution to the Montana Mavericks: What Happened at the Wedding? continuity.

ISBN-13: 978-0-373-65920-3

The Maverick's Holiday Masquerade

Copyright © 2015 by Harlequin Books S.A.

Recycling programs for this product may not exist in your area.

Printed in U.S.A.

www.Harlequin.com

The Cowboy.

Her heart thudded in her chest. Another one of those giddy waves of joy passed through her, even as the lump in her throat returned. The Cowboy! She'd wished for him and he was here, so soon after she'd made her personal vow that she could hardly believe he was real.

Yet there he was, a man she'd never seen before, holding the bridle and calming the lead horse. The Cowboy—*her* cowboy—was the most physically appealing man she'd ever seen. Tall, dark and handsome barely began to describe him, inadequate to cover the physical confidence he possessed, that aura of calm and control about him as he talked with the other men and kept the horse calm at the same time.

Who are you?

He looked right at her, as if he'd heard her ask the question. Right at her. Over the nose of the white horse, across the dozen people who milled between them, their gazes met and held.

Across the crowd, they shared a slow smile. If it was true that like attracted like, then she and this man sure were alike. When people said "two peas in a pod" to Kristen, they were invariably referring to her twin, but on this special summer day, Kristen knew that she and this man were a match, too. That smile said it all.

* * *

MONTANA MAVERICKS:
WHAT HAPPENED AT THE WEDDING?
A weekend Rust Creek Falls will never forget!

Dear Reader,

"So, what's your new book about?" You'd think I'd have an easy answer, but I get stuck. I could say it's about a man and woman falling in love, but as every reader knows, romances are about so much more. For the book you're holding now, I think the story is about assumptions. Kristen Dalton and Ryan Roarke (aka Ryan Michaels!) are wearing rose-colored glasses when they meet, and they make too many assumptions about one another as they fall in love.

Don't we all do the same? We assume certain types of people belong in certain careers. We assume small towns or big cities attract certain types, that people must be content with their lives, or that people must have greater ambitions. When their rose-colored glasses finally come off, Kristen and Ryan might just find that despite all the wrong assumptions, they've managed to fall in love with the right person!

This holiday season, I'm trying *not* to assume too much. I asked my family which traditions were the most loved, and it turns out I've been assuming they wanted me to bake more and cook more than they really did. This year, I'm only baking what we all truly want. I hope this makes the holiday less stressful and more fun—and still delicious!

I'd love to hear from you. You can drop me a private note through carocarson.com, or find me on Facebook or Twitter: @TheCaroCarson.

Cheers,

Caro Carson

Despite a no-nonsense background as a West Point graduate and US Army officer, **Caro Carson** has always treasured the happily-ever-after of a good romance novel. Now a double RITA® Award-nominated author, Caro is delighted to be living her own happily-ever-after with her husband and two children in the great state of Florida, a location that has saved the coaster-loving theme-park fanatic a fortune on plane tickets.

Books by Caro Carson

Harlequin Special Edition

Texas Rescue

Following Doctor's Orders
A Texas Rescue Christmas
Not Just a Cowboy

The Doctors MacDowell

The Bachelor Doctor's Bride
The Doctor's Former Fiancée
Doctor, Soldier, Daddy

Visit the Author Profile page
at Harlequin.com for more titles.

For my parents, Larry and Sue,
with gratitude for all the plays and ballets,
the Broadway musicals and the rock concerts,
and for setting the example by
pursuing their passion for the theater.
This theater-loving heroine had to be for you!

Chapter One

Fourth of July

"Do you see them?"

Kristen Dalton shaded her eyes with one hand as she looked up the road, but she couldn't see any hint of a horse-drawn carriage. "Sorry, sis. No sign of the bride and groom yet."

"I can't wait to see her wedding dress. The rumors have been all over the place. I've heard everything from country casual to Kardashian craziness."

Anything could be true. Although Kristen and her sister lived in a small town surrounded by ranches, technology made the world itself a small place. Even to the far northern edge of Montana, a gown from glittering Hollywood could be shipped overnight. Since the wedding dress possibilities were endless, the speculation around town had been, as well. For weeks, Kristen had been patiently listening to her twin, Kayla, list the pros and cons of every type of gown. Although today was the Fourth of July, her twin's excitement was closer to that of a kid on Christmas morning.

Kristen handed her sister her paper cup, then hopped up to perch on the top log of the split-rail fence that bordered the town park. She held out her hands for her cup and Kayla's. "Come sit with me. It could be a while. That photographer has to take pictures of a million Traub family members at the church."

Kayla climbed up to sit beside her on the railing, settling in for the wait. "What a beautiful day for their wedding."

Kristen thought it was a little too warm, nearly eighty degrees, which was as hot as things got this close to Glacier National Park. As she handed back Kayla's cup, Kristen took a healthy drink of her ice-cold wedding punch.

Thank goodness they'd decided to wear sundresses. They didn't match, of course. She and Kayla looked as identical as two peas in a pod, a phrase Kristen had been hearing for as long as she could remember, but they hadn't dressed like twins for as long as they'd been choosing their own clothes. From a distance, she supposed they looked like twins in blue dresses, but up close, they weren't alike at all.

Kayla's dress had an all-over print of tiny flowers. Her spaghetti straps were delicate, and she wore their grandmother's earrings. The shiny filigree drops were shown to their advantage on Kayla because she swept her hair up most of the time.

No one would ever see those earrings if Kristen wore them, because her hair was nearly always down.

And long. And wavy. And—*okay, I'll admit it, Mom*—always blowing in the Montana breeze and getting tangled. Their mother had despaired of keeping it neat and had given up trying somewhere around kindergarten, when Kristen had become quite adept at removing barrettes and bows.

Kristen could also admit that she'd deliberately worn blue because it made her eyes appear their bluest. Her denim halter dress always made her feel like she struck the right balance between sweet and sexy. She got smiles from the town's mavens and mavericks both. Rather than sandals, she wore her western boots. Not the solid, broken-in ones that she wore to do chores around the family ranch, but the ones with the hand-scrolled swirls in the leather. These were the boots she wore for two-stepping, waltzing and square dancing, all of which she hoped to do before, during and after tonight's fireworks.

All she needed was the right cowboy to dance with. *If only...*

If only there was a cowboy here in Rust Creek Falls that she didn't already know—and already know wasn't her type.

"I really admire Braden and Jennifer for thinking up this carriage ride," her sister said. "Their first experience as Mr. and Mrs. Traub will be private, just the two of them, as they start their journey together, figuratively, literally—"

"Briefly." Kristen nudged her in the shoulder. "The church is only two blocks away. Then we'll be right here, ready to say hi while we're really checking out the newest Mrs. Traub's gown."

Kayla shot her a look. "We're supposed to admire the bride's gown. It's expected."

"I know, I know. It'll be worth the wait, I'm sure."

"They say the best things in life are." Kayla sounded like she really meant that.

Kristen kicked the heels of her boots against the lower log railing. *Thunk, thunk.* She polished off the rest of her punch, then lifted her heavy hair from the back of her warm neck again. *Thunk, thunk.* "I hope this carriage looks amazing, because it certainly isn't a very fast way to travel."

Kayla nudged her shoulder. "I heard Sutter Traub located true white horses, and they went to someone's place south of Kalispell to borrow a two-seater surrey. Paige and Lindsay bought miles of white ribbon for it and were making bows all week."

"Wow," Kristen said, impressed at the wealth of details her sister knew. Kristen had only heard that the bride and groom were going to arrive at the park by carriage. "You've got wedding fever worse than anyone else in town, and that's saying something, considering the entire town is here for the reception."

Kristen stopped thudding her heels against the cross rail; even a twin might get annoyed at the rhythmic thumping, even an identical twin who understood Kristen's restless nature better than anyone else in the world. Squinting against the bright July sun, she joined Kayla in staring silently down Buckskin Road, past their old high school. Every kid in Rust Creek Falls had been educated there. Every kid still was. Some things in this small town never changed, and that was fine with Kristen.

She'd gone to the University of Montana, majored in theater and spent a summer as an unpaid intern in New

York City. Like Dorothy in a pair of ruby red slippers—
a role she'd played onstage at the university—she'd realized there was no place like home. Cities were great
fun to visit, but the tiny town of Rust Creek Falls under
the big sky of Montana was home. It always had been.
It always would be.

Small didn't mean boring. Things were always
changing. Their local politics could make the national
scene appear tame, but everyone had pulled together to
rebuild after a flood had wiped out a substantial portion
of the town just a couple of years ago. Old Bledsoe's
Folly, an abandoned mountain retreat, was now an upscale resort that had the town buzzing with talk about
developing the area's first ski slope.

But it was the people of Rust Creek Falls that were
the most interesting. There must be something about
Montana's famous Big Sky, because lots of folks who'd
come to help with the flood recovery or to turn Bledsoe's Folly into Maverick Manor had ended up staying,
partnered up after falling in love in Kristen's hometown.

She glanced up at that blue sky now, automatically
scanning the horizon for planes—for a certain plane. It
was a habit she'd formed earlier this year, when she'd
thought the blue sky was bringing her true love to her.
The handsome pilot of a commuter airline had turned
out to be a heartbreaker of the lowest kind. Like a sailor
with a girl in every port, he'd had a woman at every airport. Kristen still felt like an idiot for falling for him.

She got another shoulder nudge from her sister.
"Does he fly into Kalispell on weekends now?"

Leave it up to quiet Kayla to never miss a detail, not
even a glance at the sky.

Kristen wrinkled her nose. "I don't care what Captain Two-Timer does or where he flies or who he tells lies to after he lands."

"Or *to whom* he tells lies after he lands."

"You should be a writer, you know." Kristen resumed her rail-thumping. "I don't care 'to whom' he lies. It isn't to me, not anymore. 'Gee, I wish I didn't have to go. I won't be able to call you for a few days. You know I'd rather be with you, but this job is so demanding.' I was an idiot. I can't believe I couldn't see through him."

"You were in love."

"I'm not anymore." She tossed her hair back. "I'm in the mood to dance. I'm hoping for a handsome stranger or two to flirt with, but I'm not going to fall in love again."

"Not ever?"

"Not for a long while. Definitely not today."

Kayla didn't say anything for long seconds.

Kristen stopped looking for the carriage when she realized her sister was staring at her, not at the road. "What?"

"You shouldn't dare the universe to prove you wrong like that."

"Stop that. You're giving me goose bumps." Kristen jumped down from the fence, an easy drop of two feet at most, but somehow she stumbled and nearly fell. She was normally as nimble as a cat, and this sudden imbalance struck her as—funny? Yes, it was funny. It was good to giggle after that serious moment. "You stay here on carriage watch. I'll go get us some more punch. Give me your cup."

When Kayla reached down to hand her the cup, she slipped, too, and fell right into Kristen. They dissolved into giggles together, for no reason at all.

"What do you suppose is in that punch?" Kristen asked. "We only had one cup."

"I don't know, but stay here with me. Just look down that road and wait for true love to come our way."

Ryan Roarke parked his red Porsche in between two sturdy pickup trucks. The high-performance sports car belonged in Los Angeles, but this wasn't LA. In fact, Ryan had come to Montana to get away from Los Angeles. When he'd directed his assistant to reserve a luxury rental vehicle at the Glacier Park airport, he'd expected to be handed the keys to his usual Land Rover or an Audi fitted with a ski rack, the kind of rental he drove when he visited his brother in a different part of Montana, the upscale ski resort of Thunder Canyon.

This was July, however, and the roads were clear of snow, so the clerk had been enthusiastic when she'd handed him the keys to the Porsche. Ryan had attempted to return her smile when he wanted to grimace.

He grimaced now. Pulling into the packed dirt of the parking spaces at the edge of Rust Creek Falls' park in a Porsche was not what he'd had in mind for the weekend. The flashy car was so inappropriate for this rugged town, it made him look like he was having a midlife crisis. Ryan killed the powerful engine and got out, feeling like a giant at six-foot-one next to the low car. He returned the stares from a few cowboys with a hard look of his own.

Ryan knew what a midlife crisis looked like—too many of his fellow attorneys blew their children's inheritances on sports cars in an effort to replace their children's mothers with starlets—but he didn't know what one felt like. He was *not* having a midlife crisis.

He was only thirty-three, for starters, and a confirmed bachelor. He wasn't trying to appear more wealthy or powerful or attractive to women than he already was.

As the second generation of well-known attorneys in Los Angeles, Ryan already owned the sports cars, the Rolex, the hand-tailored suits. Physical intimidation had a subliminal effect even in a courtroom, and Ryan kept himself in fighting shape by boxing with exclusive trainers and surfing on exclusive beaches. When it came to young, blonde starlets finding him attractive, he didn't even have to try.

This was definitely not a midlife crisis.

So why am I standing in the smallest of towns in a landlocked state more than one thousand miles away from home?

He was supposed to be on a yacht, slowly getting sloshed with his fellow millionaires, drinking top-shelf mojitos while waiting for the sun to set over the Pacific and for the city of Los Angeles to blow an obscene amount of money on a fireworks display worthy of a Hollywood movie. One Laker Girl, in particular, was quite upset he'd canceled those plans. But the government had closed the courts of law on Friday for the holiday weekend, and for the past two years, whenever Ryan found himself with a chance to take a few days off, he'd found himself taking those days off in Montana.

The reason he'd first set foot in Big Sky Country was his brother. Shane Roarke had gained fame as a celebrity chef, a man whose dynamic personality and culinary skill had combined to give him the keys to the world. Shane had opened restaurants all over that world, but when it came to choosing one place to live, he'd chosen Montana.

Shane, like Ryan, was adopted. Shane had found his birth family in Thunder Canyon. He'd found a pair of half brothers, a baker's dozen of cousins—and the love of his life. She'd been working right under his nose at his own restaurant in the Thunder Canyon resort.

None of that would be happening for Ryan. Not in Montana, and not anywhere else on the planet. Unlike Shane, Ryan hadn't been adopted at birth. He'd been almost four years old, too young to have many memories of his birth mother, but old enough to have retained an image or two, impressions.

Feelings.

And that one clear moment in time: watching his mother voluntarily walk away from him, forever.

No, there would never be an embrace from a happy second family for him. He was loyal only to one family: the Roarkes. His parents, Christa and Gavin Roarke, his older brother Shane, his younger sister Maggie.

It was Maggie who lived here in Rust Creek Falls, some three hundred miles even farther north than Thunder Canyon. Maggie was married now, and she'd given birth to her first baby less than three months ago.

The Fourth of July wasn't a big family holiday, not like Thanksgiving or Christmas. Between the LA traffic to the airport, the security checks, and the need to change planes in order to cross one thousand miles, Montana was no weekend jaunt. No one was expected to travel for nine or ten hours to see family for a day in July. And yet, Maggie had mentioned over the phone that the whole town would be celebrating the wedding for a couple Ryan vaguely knew from a previous trip, and he'd booked a flight.

Another moment in time, another feeling: *A wedding in Rust Creek Falls? I should be there.*

He was acting irrationally, following a hunch. Was that any worse behavior than the attorneys who really were having midlife crises?

Maggie had told him the wedding would be in the church, a formal affair with five bridesmaids and men in tuxedos. Accordingly, Ryan was wearing a suit and tie. He owned a few tuxedos, of course, but since the wedding was in the afternoon and he was one of an entire town of guests, he'd assumed wearing black tie would be too much.

As Ryan made his way from the parking lot to the main part of the park, he returned a few curious but courteous nods from the locals. His assumption about the tux being overkill had clearly been correct, but even his suit was too much. The reception was also the town's Fourth of July community barbecue. Ryan felt exactly like what he was, an overdressed city slicker, standing in a grassy field that was dotted with picnic blankets and populated by cowboys in their jeans and cowgirls in their sundresses.

He stopped near the temporary stage and wooden dance floor. The bride and groom hadn't arrived yet, but the band was warming up and the drinks were being served. An old man came toward him, going out of his way just to offer Ryan a cup of wedding punch in a paper cup. Amused, Ryan thanked him, realizing the old-timer must have thought he looked like he needed a drink, standing alone as he was.

He was alone, but only because Maggie and her husband were back at their house, hoping their baby would take a nap so they could return for the fireworks later. Being alone didn't mean Ryan was lonely.

Ryan took a swig of the wedding punch, then immediately wished he hadn't. It was a god-awful sweet concoction with sparkling wine thrown in, something he'd never drink under almost any other circumstance. Worse, he couldn't just pour the stuff out on the grass. In a small town like this one, he was as likely to be standing near the person who made the punch as not. Some doting grandma or an earnest young lady had probably mixed the juice and wine, and the odds were good that if Ryan dumped it out, she'd see him do it. He'd break some proud punch maker's heart.

If there was one thing Ryan was not, it was a heartbreaker. His Laker Girl, for example, was irritated at losing a yacht outing, but she wasn't heartbroken. He kept his relationships painless, his connections surface-deep. In LA, it seemed right. Today, here in this park, it seemed...too little.

He polished off the punch, but on his way to the industrial-size trash can, he passed the punch table and found himself accosted by a trio of sweet little grannies.

"Well, don't you look nice?"

"Are you waiting on somebody? A handsome young man like you must have a date for this wedding."

"It's nearly eighty degrees. You must be ready to melt in that jacket, not that you don't look very fine."

He wasn't overheated. In Los Angeles, the temperature would easily reach one hundred, and he'd still wear a suit between his office and the courthouse. It took more than a reading on a thermometer to make him lose his cool.

Still, he appreciated their maternal concern. Their

faces were creased with laugh lines, and all three of them had sparkling blue eyes that had probably been passed down from the Norwegians and Germans who'd settled here centuries ago. It was like being fussed over by three kindly characters from one of Grimm's fairy tales.

"Here, son, let me refill your cup."

"No, thank you." Ryan waved off the punch bowl ladle.

All three women jerked to attention, then looked at him through narrowed eyes, their fairy-tale personas taking on the aura of determined villainesses.

"Don't be foolish, dear. The day is hot and this punch is cold."

This was Montana, land of grizzly bears as well as grannies. At the moment, it seemed like there might not be much difference between the two groups. When confronted by a bear, one should let it have its way. Ryan forced another smile as the punch pushers refilled his cup.

"Thank you very much." He raised his paper cup in a toasting gesture, took a healthy swig to make them happy and continued on his way.

To where? Just where did he have to go?

To a trash can. He had nowhere else to be, nothing else to do, no one else to see.

His vision burst into stars, like he'd been hit in the boxing ring, a TKO. He put his hand out to steady himself, the wooden fence rough under his palm. He wasn't drunk. It wasn't possible on a cup of juice-diluted sparkling wine. And yet he felt…he felt…

Good God, he felt like garbage.

Useless.

Maggie was with her husband. Shane was with his wife. Even his parents were together back in California, planning their retirement, ready to travel and spend time together as Christa and Gavin after decades tirelessly fulfilling the roles of Mom and Dad.

Lonely.

One thousand miles he'd traveled, and for what? To be a stranger in a strange land? He looked around, keeping his grip on the split-rail fence. Everywhere, everyone had someone. Children had grandparents. Husbands had wives. Awkward teenagers had each other. The teen girls were toying with their hair, whispering and talking and looking at the boys. The boys stood with their arms crossed over their chests, testing their fledgling cowboy swagger, but they stood in a cluster with other boys with crossed arms, all being independent together.

All being independent, together. That was what this town was about. Ryan had first come here after a flood had decimated the southern half of the town. His sister had been helping process insurance claims in the town hall. Maggie was so efficient Ryan hadn't been needed the weekend he'd arrived to help. Instead, he'd picked up a spare pair of work gloves and started using his muscles instead of his brains, picking up the pieces, literally, of someone's broken dream.

Without a lot of conversation, he'd joined a cluster of men and women as they'd each picked up one brick, one board, one metal window frame to toss in a Dumpster before reaching for the next. One by one, each piece of debris had been cleared away. Independently but together, he and the others removed the remains of an entire house in a day, leaving the lot ready for a fresh building and a new dream.

With a few nods and handshakes, all the men and women had gone their separate ways after sunset, to eat and rest and do it all over again the next day. Ryan had never been part of something so profound.

He stared at the split-rail fence under his hand. That was why he kept coming back. For one day, he'd belonged. No one had cared which law firm he was with, which part of LA he could afford to live in, which clients had invited him onto their yachts. He'd been part of this community, no questions asked, and he'd liked it.

But now, they don't need me.

He rejected that thought, hearing in it the echo of a pitiful little boy whose mother had decided he was no longer needed in her life. Rejected that emotion as he had rejected it so many times before. He refused to be an unwanted child. He was a Roarke, a powerful attorney from a powerful family, and when he wanted something, no one could stop him from achieving it.

He just needed to know what he wanted.

The drunken, emotional craziness cleared from his mind as he kept staring at his hand, still gripping the solid wood railing. Slowly, he lifted his gaze, following the line of the fence as it stretched along the perimeter of the park. He could hardly believe the direction his own mind was taking, but his thoughts were heading straight toward one idea. What if he chose a new path in life? What if he came to Montana for more than a long weekend? Could he live here? Would he feel like he belonged, or would he always be skirting along the outside of the close-knit community?

His visual run along the length of the fence was interrupted a hundred yards away by two women in blue dresses who were sitting on the railing, their backs to the people of the town. The one with the loose, long hair threw her head back and laughed at something the other woman said, happy although she was on the outskirts of the party.

Happy, because she's not alone.

Shane and Maggie were happy in Montana, too, because they were not alone. Marriage and parenthood were sobering concepts for him. He didn't think he'd be very good at either one, and he didn't particularly have a burning desire to try, either. He let go of the fence and headed back toward the Porsche, loosening his tie as he went. Maybe he had come to Montana looking for something, but it hadn't been for love.

If he made such a drastic change, if he gave up LA for a life in a small town, he'd do so on his own terms. This was about a different standard of living, a different pace of life. There was only one way to find out if this town could meet his terms, and that was to try it on for size. Just for today, he was going to act like he belonged here. He'd eat some barbecue, dance with some local girls and decide if this community of extended families and battered pickup trucks was really richer than his moneyed life in LA.

If he decided it was, then he'd develop and execute a plan for responsibly resigning from Roarke and Associates in Los Angeles and moving permanently to Montana.

What if they don't like me here, now that they don't need me?

He shoved the boyishly insecure emotion aside as he opened the Porsche's trunk to get to his suitcase. The Porsche had its trunk in the front of the car and the engine in the back, making it just as unusual as

Ryan himself in this humble parking lot. The Porsche was doomed to always be different. But he, with a simple change of clothes, could make himself fit in. He'd brought the jeans he usually wore to ride ATVs in Thunder Canyon and the boots he'd worn when he'd helped out after the flood.

If the town rejected him this time, if he was treated like he was no longer wanted now that the flood was a receding memory, then no harm done. He'd lived through rejection before. He could take any heartache this town could dish out.

He took off his Rolex and tossed it into the trunk before slamming the red metal shut.

Chapter Two

"Well, it won't be long now. The band's tuning up."

Thank goodness. That giggly buzz from the powerful punch had started wearing off, giving way to a different sensation. After a few tipsy laughs with her sister, Kristen now felt more than sober. She felt almost somber, as she shifted her seat on the increasingly uncomfortable wood rail.

Her life needed to get on the right track. Things weren't right. Pieces were missing. She was twenty-five, a college graduate with a passion for the theater, yet she spent her days running to the feed store and performing the same ranch chores she'd been assigned in junior high. Not that she wanted to lose her roots—her family, the ranch, this town—but she wanted more. An outlet for her theatrical passion—something that was hard to find in her hometown. An outlet for real passion, too, someone to lose her head and her heart over—someone who wouldn't trample them this time.

This bad mood was probably just because a plane had flown overhead, reminding her that a good man was hard to find. Maybe she envied her pilot for having a home base but the freedom to fly and explore. If only he hadn't been exploring with other women in other towns...

Jeez, she was spiraling down into a full-blown pity party.

The band began playing its first song of the afternoon. Kristen looked over her shoulder toward the empty wooden dance floor in the distance. If no one else started dancing, she'd get the party started and be grateful for the chance. If there was one thing that could shake Kristen out of the blues, it was a party. And man, was she feeling blue.

Stupid airplane.

The wedding carriage appeared at the end of the block with a flutter of white ribbons and the tossing of a horse's snowy white mane. If Cinderella had been a cowgirl, this would have been her glass carriage.

"Oh, wow."

"Wow."

There were no other words between the sisters. As the surrey rolled steadily toward them, Kristen swallowed around a sudden but definite lump in her throat.

The closer the carriage came, the more clearly she saw the faces of the couple on the high bench. The groom, a man born and bred in Rust Creek Falls like Kristen herself, was transformed. Kristen felt she'd never seen Braden Traub before. Wearing a tuxedo and black cowboy hat, he held the reins loosely in his hands and kept his face turned toward his bride. Whatever she was saying, he found fascinating. He had eyes only for her and never looked at the horses, and yet, had those horses bolted, Kristen knew he would have had them back under his control within seconds, never allowing his bride to be in danger.

"I want what they have," her sister said, reverence in her quiet tone.

"Me, too."

With a love like that, she could branch out, she could fly, she could be fearless. A love like that would be her home base, the heartbeat at the center that made everything else come alive.

Kristen laid her head on Kayla's shoulder. Her sister was supposed to be the serious twin, but Kristen suddenly felt like crying, completely undone by the romance of the moment, by what was possible between a man and woman, by what she'd never experienced herself.

I want a cowboy, capable and strong, who has eyes only for me, who loves only me, 'til death do us part.

She loved her family. She loved her hometown. And someday, she silently vowed, she would love a cowboy who was honest and true. *If only...*

If only she could find the right cowboy.

"No more city slickers for me," Kristen whispered. "I'll have the real deal, or I'll stay single forever."

"To true love." Kayla raised her cup in a toast.

Kristen knew Kayla was trying to cheer her up, so she straightened and lifted her cup. "To true love. Too bad we're out of actual punch for this toast."

"It still counts."

The carriage had been noticed by other people as

it drew closer to the park entrance. Kristen and Kayla jumped down from the fence to join the growing crowd as they followed the carriage into the heart of the park. The bride and groom's tête-à-tête was over as Braden pulled the team to a stop amid applause, good-natured catcalls about what had taken so long and a flurry of activity as the bride gathered up her skirts and bouquet, preparing to get down from the high surrey bench.

"Looks like she went traditional with a sweetheart neckline. I'm going to the other side to get a better look at her dress, okay?"

"Have fun," Kristen said as Kayla slipped through the small crowd.

Braden tied off the reins and set the brake, but for added safety amid the noisy well-wishers, two cowboys held the bridles of the white horses as Braden jumped down from the surrey. One cowboy was Sutter Traub, the town's own horse whisperer, and the other was...

The Cowboy.

Kristen's heart thudded in her chest. Another one of those giddy waves of joy passed through her, even as the lump in her throat returned. The Cowboy! She'd wished for him and he was here, so soon after she'd made her personal vow, she could hardly believe he was real.

Yet there he was, a man she'd never seen before, holding the bridle and calming the lead horse as Braden handed his bride down from the surrey. The Cowboy— *her* cowboy—was the most physically appealing man she'd ever seen. Tall, dark and handsome barely began to describe him, inadequate to cover the physical confidence he possessed as he talked with the other men and kept the horse calm at the same time. The Cowboy had an air of authority that had surely come from a lifetime of handling anything that land or livestock could throw at a man.

Kristen stepped a little to one side, and the crowd parted just enough that she could check him out from his boots and jeans—check and check—to his white button-down shirt. It looked a little dressy for the picnic; he'd probably been at the church for the ceremony. He'd cuffed up the long sleeves, revealing strong forearms.

He was tan, but so were most of the ranchers who worked outdoors. Even the summer sun couldn't lighten his nearly black hair, which he wore short, but not shorn. It was long enough that she could see a bit of a wave in it, and she knew it would feel glorious when she could run her fingers through it. When he was hers, she'd have the right to touch him and casually brush his hair back from his forehead.

Her gaze traveled past his broad shoulders to the strong hands that held the bridle. When he was hers, she'd have the right to touch him anywhere. Everywhere.

Her fingers practically tingled in anticipation.

He wore no cowboy hat, but that wasn't unusual. Half the cowboys didn't wear one when they weren't working. A lot of the local guys wore ball caps with dumb fishing mottos on them, but not her cowboy. He looked too classy for that. He looked...

She couldn't put her tingling finger on it, but he didn't quite look like any of the cowboys from around Rust Creek Falls.

He's not from around here, that's why.

Kristen would have noticed him long ago if he were a local.

Who are you?

He looked right at her, as if he'd heard her ask the question. Over the nose of the white horse, across the dozen people who milled between them, their gazes met and held.

The people and the picnic and the party disappeared. Kristen felt only the heat in his dark brown eyes. He checked her out as thoroughly as she'd been checking him out, his gaze moving across her bare shoulders, down the V of her halter dress, taking in her boots with a brief quirk of his lips. She didn't miss it, because she hadn't looked away for a second. She was no shrinking violet. When he realized she was still watching him, he lifted a brow. She tossed her hair back and shrugged one bare shoulder.

Across the crowd, they shared a slow smile. If it was true that like attracted like, then she and this man sure were alike. When people said "two peas in a pod" to Kristen, they were invariably referring to her twin, but on this special summer day, Kristen knew that she and this man were a match, too. That smile said it all.

Without warning, the horse he was holding threw its head up. The Cowboy lost his grip on the bridle and took a head-butt to the jaw. Of course, he had the bridle back in hand and the horse steady in a second, but as his dark brown eyes met Kristen's once more, his mouth quirked again in a bit of a sheepish smile.

Kristen wanted to toss her head like the snowy white horse. *What do you know? I just made a cowboy lose control of a horse.*

With a self-satisfied smile, Kristen turned toward the pavilion and the punch table. It was time to get two fresh cups and introduce herself to the man of her dreams.

* * *

Ryan rubbed his jaw as he moved with the rest of the wedding party toward the stage.

That horse had hit him as hard as the best boxer he'd ever faced down in the ring. Ryan was grateful that he knew how to take a punch. He'd managed to stay on his feet, so he hadn't looked like a complete fool in front of the exquisite woman he'd been so thoroughly distracted by. He *hoped* he hadn't looked like a fool. She'd disappeared into the crowd.

He'd find her again. The crowd here wasn't big enough for someone to get lost permanently, a point definitely in favor of small towns at the moment. He scanned the people edging the dance floor, looking for her unusual blend of delicate features and a bold gaze.

The lead singer of the band spoke into the microphone. "Ladies and gentlemen, may I have your attention please? I'd like to turn the stage over to the mayor of Rust Creek Falls, Collin Traub."

Another Traub. Was everyone in the town related to the bride and groom? And, by birth and by blood, to Ryan's own brother?

As a man about Ryan's age took the mike amid a round of applause, everyone turned to face the stage. Ryan kept looking through the crowd, scanning the backs of the heads of the people in front of him, looking for one particular woman's long hair.

The attorney side of himself, which was practically the only side he had, yanked his attention back to the stage. If he was seriously considering a move to this town, he ought to be evaluating the mayor. Local government would have a huge impact on the growth of the town and the requirements for operating a business. He couldn't prosper in a town that elected inflexible or unqualified people to office. Ryan focused on the mayor, who still wore his tuxedo as part of the wedding party, a tuxedo with a bolo tie instead of a bow tie, of course. The men around here were never far from their cowboy roots, even in their formal attire. The mayor's welcome speech was sensible, friendly and, that most appreciated trait of all speeches, short.

Like Ryan's attention span. He couldn't focus on anything but seeing that woman again. The sun had highlighted her hair when he'd seen her, framing her in a halo of light. He was looking for a shade of brown that shone with gold, like caramel or honey or something appealing he'd find in one of his brother's kitchens.

Unbelievable. He was turning into a poet. Beautiful, long hair was hardly a rarity where he came from, but Ryan would bet a million dollars that he could bury his hands in his mystery woman's hair and not have to politely avoid the anchors of fake hair extensions. So many women in Hollywood paid a fortune to look like they had the kind of hair that his boot-wearing beauty probably had gained through healthy living on a ranch.

In a flash, he saw himself burying his hands in her hair, holding her reverently as she gazed up at him from the pillow, her happiness a part of his pleasure as—

Get a grip, Ryan.

He needed to snap out of this. This day was turning strange, whether it was from the strain of work and travel, the strangeness of ruminating over his siblings' marriages or the sight of a bride and groom, he couldn't say. Maybe it was the higher elevation or the cleaner air or that damned syrupy wedding punch, but he felt off.

The mayor called the bride and groom to the stage for

the best man's toast. Ryan saw the three fairy-tale grannies circulating in the crowd, coming toward him with trays of paper cups, making sure everyone who didn't already have a drink in hand accepted one of theirs.

Absolutely not. Ryan Roarke, attorney at law, was not going to drink punch and spin ridiculous fantasies about a cowgirl he hadn't even met. He turned on his heel and headed away from the stage.

"Were you looking for this? I think you're going to need it."

Ryan stopped abruptly, face to face with the cowgirl herself. Had he been heading straight for her, or had she stepped into his path? Either way, she was right here, stunningly beautiful in denim and sunshine.

She held out a cup and nodded toward the stage behind him. "It's time for the toast."

From her, he'd take the punch. He'd probably stand here and drink water from the river Styx, as long as he could keep looking at her. She looked right back, her blue eyes and heart-shaped face framed by that hair he so keenly wanted to touch.

"I'm Kristen," she said with a smile.

He nodded gravely, aware that this was an introduction he'd remember.

"Ryan," he said, and he suddenly didn't care about Montana or Hollywood, about mayors and law firms. The only thing he cared about was getting to know the woman who smiled at him in a green park on the Fourth of July. She was worth traveling a thousand miles.

"You're not from around here, are you?" she asked.

"No, I'm not." Now that he'd decided what he wanted, he could relax. He found himself smiling at her—with her—without any effort at all. "But I could be."

The best man finished his toast. "To the new Mr. and Mrs. Braden Traub."

The crowd around them cheered and raised their drinks to toast the happy couple. Ryan tapped his cup to Kristen's, then watched her over the rim of his cup as they drank to the newlyweds' happiness.

The band struck up a song, a country-western ballad for the bride and groom's first dance, and the lovely Kristen turned to face the dance floor.

With the taste of that sweet punch lingering on his tongue, Ryan looked at the faces of the townspeople who were looking at the newlyweds, faces that were young and old and in between. He could practically feel the goodwill and best wishes being directed toward the center of the dance floor as the bride and groom danced alone. Where were the murmured whispers about the prenuptial agreement? The bets that this marriage wouldn't last longer than the bride's previous two or the groom's last three?

Ryan glanced down at the beautiful woman beside him. Her profile was not only pure physical perfection, but the expression on her face looked to him to be genuinely pure, as well, as open and honest as her friends' and neighbors' faces. He rubbed his still-aching jaw in disbelief. He'd had to see this to believe it, the possibility that an entire town could be truly wishing this couple a lifetime of happiness. If he wanted to fit in here, he'd have to leave some of his skepticism in LA.

The song came to an end, and Kristen bit the edge of her cup in her perfect white teeth so her hands were free to applaud with the rest of the crowd.

"Allow me." Ryan tugged the cup from her, charmed by her unselfconscious smile. He slid her empty cup inside his own, then turned to put them down on the nearest picnic table.

The lead singer of the band was doubling as the master of ceremonies. "Everyone is invited to join in for this next dance. For every couple who gets on the dance floor, the bride and groom will get another year of happiness, so don't be shy. Find your partners."

The fiddle player began the first notes of a country-western song in the clear one-two-three rhythm of a waltz.

Ryan didn't know how to two-step or boot-scoot or do any kind of country dancing, but a waltz was a waltz, whether it was danced under the chandeliers of a ballroom or on temporary wood planking in a park. He could fit in here, on the dance floor with the citizens of Rust Creek Falls, and he could waltz with the prettiest cowgirl of them all.

"May I have this dance?" he asked.

"You may." Kristen took her place in his arms with a graceful swirl of her denim dress. They began to move as one.

There was nothing that satisfied Ryan's sense of irony more than holding a beautiful woman in a ballroom dance. It seemed so civilized on the surface, when it was really a way to bring a man and a woman's bodies in sync. While they performed the prescribed moves of the centuries-old waltz, he could touch the smooth skin of her upper back, left bare by the halter dress. He could feel the incredible softness of her hair brushing his wrist as they turned in smooth circles. He could hold her so close that they stepped between each other's legs, graceful movements of her booted feet between his own.

"I love the waltz even more than the two-step," she

said, civilized small talk made while her thighs brushed against his.

"I do, too." Of course, he only knew the waltz, not the two-step, but he'd watch and learn the two-step in record time today. He intended to dance as much as possible with Kristen. This was where he wanted to be, but more importantly, this was the woman with whom he wanted to be. She moved with him effortlessly, lightly, wonderfully. The moment in time seemed perfect.

As if this dance were destined to be.

No. He didn't believe in things like destiny. Men and women had to carve their own lives out of the circumstances they were dealt. As beautiful as the woman in his arms was, as expressive as her eyes were and as easily as her smile came, it was still absurd to think she'd come into his life today because of destiny.

It was even more absurd that he was debating the possibility.

It had to be the wedding. The music. The damned effect of that punch. This was just an average town, a simple song, an average band. There was nothing special about this waltz, and the woman he shared it with was merely a pretty country girl. Those were facts, not fate.

He was an attorney, a man of letters. Like his parents, he believed in laws and rules, not in mystical interpretations of life.

But Mom, I'm not really a Roarke.

Oh, but you are. I think you were always meant to be my son, and I was always meant to be your mother.

The memory caught him by surprise. Did his analytical adoptive mother truly believe in fate, or had she said those words to comfort a boy who'd never forgotten being left behind?

"Are you okay?"

Kristen's soft question brought him back to reality. He gave her a polite, reassuring smile that was little more than a reflex.

"Yes, I'm fine."

How odd that she'd asked. He hadn't changed the rhythm of their dancing or the way he was holding her as he'd remembered his mother's words about destiny. On the surface, everything was the same, all smooth skin, smooth steps, synchronicity. And yet, Kristen had noticed his subtle change in mood.

She was more than a pretty country girl, and he couldn't fool himself otherwise. There was something special about her. This day had become so much more than a weekend away from the rat race. This town, this celebration, this woman all combined to make Ryan feel like he was standing at the brink of something new. Did she feel it, too?

He'd known her for minutes. He couldn't ask her if she believed in destiny, but he could hold her as the band played, so he lost himself in her blue eyes as they waltzed together under the big Montana sky.

The Cowboy didn't seem inclined to make small talk, and she loved dancing too much to want to chatter about nothing when she could be enjoying the music and the motion, so they danced in silence as one song led to the next.

Occasionally, though, she noticed someone on the dance floor would seem to recognize Ryan, and they'd exchanged a friendly nod.

Who are you? Where did you come from?

She was half-afraid to ask. He was too perfect for

her—he even wanted to dance every song, just like she did—so she could almost imagine she'd conjured him up. Like a figment of her imagination, he could disappear as easily as he'd arrived.

Sooner than she would have liked, the band stopped playing and the wedding cake was cut with the usual ceremony. It went without saying that after being so in tune with Ryan on the dance floor, they'd take their cake slices and walk in step toward one of the many card tables that had been set up under the park's shade trees.

Dancing had been all about communicating with movement, but Kristen had no desire to sit across from the man and eat wedding cake in silence.

"Will you be in town long?" she asked, jumping in with both feet and asking the most important question first. Her brothers would probably shake their heads and say she was being too bold again, but her sister would probably tell her she'd make a good journalist, getting right to the point.

"Just until tomorrow." Ryan set his plate aside and gave her his full attention, arms crossed on the table, gaze on her face.

Shivers ran down her spine. Hadn't she vowed to find a man who paid attention to her and only her?

Her sister had been so serious as they'd sat on the fence, telling Kristen she shouldn't dare the universe with her declaration about not falling in love today. If the universe had decided to prove Kristen wrong by setting the perfect man in front of her as a temptation— well, heck, that wasn't much of a punishment. She'd said she wouldn't fall in love, but a girl would be crazy not to reconsider after meeting a man like Ryan.

She flipped her hair back over her shoulder to keep

it out of the white icing. "What did you mean when I asked you if you were from around here, and you said you could be?"

"It's a thought I've been entertaining. It might be time to get out of the fast lane and settle down, somewhere away from the madding crowds. I like Montana."

She licked a little frosting off her finger as she listened. Not a lot of cowboys would describe their lives as being in the fast lane.

"I've visited a few places in Montana over the past couple of years," he said, "but right now, Rust Creek Falls looks just about perfect."

He was looking right at her. Another shiver went down her spine, and she decided the sensation was as delicious as the cake. She was already half in love with Ryan. He was handsome and humorous, with a cowboy's good manners and rock-hard body, and most of all, he seemed to be interested in everything she had to say. If he was considering a permanent move to Rust Creek Falls, the universe had won the dare. She'd fall in love today and be happy that the universe had known better than she had.

"Are you a Traub?" he asked.

"No, I'm a Dalton."

"Good. I was starting to think everyone was a Traub except me."

It could have been her overactive actress's imagination, but he'd said that line with a touch of wistfulness.

"Don't feel too left out. There are oodles of Daltons and Crawfords and Stricklands here, too. You don't have to be a Traub to live in Rust Creek Falls."

One of the Traubs in question passed near their table,

Collin Traub, the mayor, to be exact. He nodded at Ryan, who hesitated just a moment before nodding back.

"You know Collin?" Kristen asked. That was excellent. The more ties Ryan had to this town, the more reasons he had to stay.

"Collin who?"

"The man you just nodded at."

"No, not really." He looked away from her toward Collin, then glanced around the other tables, but his gaze didn't stop on anyone in particular.

He knew no one, then. That could be a lonely feeling. Kristen remembered feeling lost on campus when she'd first arrived at the University of Montana. The modest city of Missoula had seemed like a giant metropolis of heartless strangers.

She didn't want Ryan to feel that way, not in her town. She slid his discarded plate back in front of him, took his fork and scooped up a chunk from the best part of the slice, the corner between the top and side that had the most frosting. Maybe a little sugar would bring the smile back to his face.

She held the fork up. "Here, eat this. You can't let homemade cake go to waste."

He didn't smile. One brow lifted slightly at her impulsive gesture. She hadn't thought it through, but if she'd expected him to take the fork from her, she'd been wrong. Instead, with his intense gaze never leaving her face, he leaned forward and ate the bite off the fork as she held it.

It was a move for lovers. There was an intimacy to feeding someone. She could imagine that mouth on her skin, tasting her, taking his time, savoring the moment...

Kristen sat back in the metal chair and lifted the hair off the back of her neck. The heat of the day hadn't dissipated, although it was getting close to suppertime, but she knew the real reason she was warm, and it had to do with a man who was just a bit older, just a bit more self-possessed, just a bit more devilish, than the men she usually dated. The universe had outdone itself.

She leaned forward once more, determined to match Ryan's confidence. "Collin seemed to recognize you, even if you don't know him."

Ryan nodded once, a crisp acknowledgment of her observation. "I'm surprised. I didn't think anyone around here would recognize me."

The proverbial lightbulb went off over Kristen's head. What kind of cowboy talked about crowds and fast lanes? What kind of cowboy got recognized by people who were strangers to him?

A cowboy who starred in the rodeo, that was who. Collin Traub had once been a rodeo rider, and he recognized Ryan.

In ninth grade, Kristen had gone through her rodeo phase. She'd been able to name all the best cutting horses and recite the bloodlines of all the barrel-racing champions, but even then, she'd been more interested in boys than livestock. She'd been able to name the most handsome bull riders as well as the most noble horses. She'd begged her parents to drive her all the way to the Missoula Stampede. Afterward, she'd cut photos of her favorite cowboys out of the color program and taped them to the inside of her locker.

She'd outgrown that infatuation. Cowboy crushes had given way to movie star mania, and she'd left the ranch to taste life on the stage. Now everything seemed to be coming full circle. Here she was, eating wedding cake on the Fourth of July with a rodeo rider. The Cowboy. *Her* Cowboy.

Bravo, Universe. Bravo.

Since the professional rodeo circuit ran nearly all its events in July and August, she wasn't surprised Ryan had to leave town tomorrow. It was only surprising he'd been able to stop here today. He'd hoped Rust Creek Falls would give him a break from his everyday life in the fast lane. When people recognized Ryan, he returned all their nods politely, but he hadn't been striking up conversations or handing out autographs. He didn't want to play up his life on the professional circuit obviously.

She wasn't about to ask him about his life on the rodeo circuit, either. Her days as a fourteen-year-old fan were long behind her. Now she was the woman who'd fed a man cake while he'd devoured her with his eyes. That man was the person she wanted to get to know.

She only had today to do it. One day for him to decide if he'd ever come back to Rust Creek Falls—or rather, one day for her to decide if she ought to convince him.

One day that could decide the rest of their lives.

Chapter Three

Kristen missed the feel of having Ryan's arms around her, but even the most die-hard dancers had to take a break when the band stopped playing.

As the next band set up its equipment, Kristen got to know more about Ryan than the clean smell of his dress shirt and the way their bodies fit together in a slow dance. Sitting together on a corner of the stage, they discussed everything from favorite sports teams to favorite seasons. She loved the Green Bay Packers and Christmas. He preferred the New York Yankees and summer. He was the middle child of three; she was the baby of five—even if she was only separated from number four by a few minutes. His siblings didn't live in the same state as he did; her entire family lived in the same town.

"In other words," Kristen said, "we have everything in common."

"A perfectly logical conclusion." Ryan kept his expression perfectly serious, too, although she knew he was teasing her.

"It is." She polished off her punch and set her cup down, prepared to check off her conclusions one by one on her fingers. "We both enjoy watching professional sports. We each have one sister. We each have at least one older brother. We talk to our families all the time."

That made four. She wiggled her pinky finger, the last one she hadn't checked off. "And we both love to dance. Like I said, we've got everything in common."

His slow smile was just about the sexiest thing about him, and considering everything about him was sexy, that was saying something. "I have no objection to any of that. But for the sake of accuracy, and to give myself an excuse to keep watching a beautiful woman as she makes an animated argument, I have to point out that our preferred seasons are opposites."

"That is a fact." Kristen was never one to back down from a challenge. She lowered her voice. "Having one thing we don't agree on keeps it…interesting."

His gaze dropped to her mouth. He was interested, all right.

"Differences can be good. For example, you're a boy. I'm a girl." She pointed at his chest, then at hers, his gaze dropping farther, down to where she pressed her finger to her heart. "You're summer, I'm Christmas."

Just as their eyes had met over the head of that white horse, his gaze suddenly left her finger and focused right on her. He looked serious for real this time, no joke to it. "I believe if anyone could make Christmas better, it would be you."

Kristen leaned in a little closer. "If every Fourth of

July could be spent with you, I'd start to look forward to summer as soon as the first snow fell."

He was going to kiss her. Right here, sitting on the edge of the stage in the middle of the town's celebration, he was going to kiss her, and she felt her heart beating under her own fingertip in anticipation.

But he didn't. In silence, he looked at her for one second longer, then lifted his cup to her in a salute, and downed his punch.

"Hi, Kristen."

She looked up to see one of the guys from her high school drama club days standing over her with his guitar.

"My band's on for the next hour. Make sure you clap even if we suck, okay?"

"You'll be great." Kristen stood along with Ryan, and yielded the stage with a wave of her hand. "It's all yours. Break a leg."

The dance floor began filling up again. She spotted Kayla dancing with someone else Kristen hadn't seen in a while, one of their brothers' friends who'd been a few years ahead of them in high school.

High school. Again. She was twenty-five. She didn't want her life to revolve around high school. Hadn't she evolved since then?

Yes, of course she had. She was just overthinking everything.

There was something in the air today. The town seemed different somehow. Maybe because a police officer she didn't recognize had walked past her, heading toward the fountain and the sounds of a fight, although public brawls were rare in Rust Creek Falls. Maybe because a high-stakes poker game had kicked off at the Ace in the Hole bar, and lots of rowdier folk were drifting that way. Members of the wedding party were sneaking off, too, headed for the park exit, where the groom's truck was now parked in preparation for the getaway.

A getaway. It sounded appealing on one level, but she'd already been there, done that. She'd gotten a college degree, even lived in New York City one summer, and then returned to Rust Creek Falls by choice. She wasn't stuck here; she was happy here. People visited and ended up staying permanently, which was proof enough that the town was great. If the Cowboy settled down here, maybe she'd feel more settled herself.

"Where do you want to go?" Ryan asked.

Kristen almost laughed at the timing. "Is that a trick question? Do you mean where do I want to go in life or just in the next five minutes?"

"They say the journey of a lifetime starts with a single step." A smile teased the corners of his mouth. "I've always thought that put a lot of pressure on choosing where to step."

"Let's be daring and step this way, then." She stood shoulder to shoulder with him and deliberately raised her knee high, then took a giant step in the direction of the fence where she'd sat with her sister, waiting for true love to arrive.

Those moments with her sister seemed prophetic now. Her emotions seemed wild and free today, swinging from a kind of drunken silliness to intensely important. Through it all, she'd had Ryan's arm around her on the dance floor, Ryan sitting across from her at the table, Ryan walking beside her now, matching her stride for stride after that first silly step.

"I think the bride and groom are going to make a break for it," Kristen said. "We can wave goodbye from the fence." The fireworks wouldn't begin until after ten since the sun set so late in July, but Kristen had noticed the newest Traub couple saying goodbye to their bridesmaids and groomsmen.

"I guess they're not too worried about seeing fireworks tonight," she said. "Maybe they'll watch them from the balcony of Maverick Manor. That's where they're staying. They'll fly out tomorrow on their honeymoon."

"I'm sure they'll see fireworks tonight." Ryan kept his serious poker face in place as they reached the fence.

She did a little Groucho Marx imitation, wagging her eyebrows and pretending she held a cigar. "Fireworks? Is that what the kids are calling it these days?"

Ryan gave her a boost to sit on the top rail. His laughter was as warm and masculine as the brief touch of his hands on her waist. He stayed on the ground, leaning against the fence, and crossed his ankles as he settled in for the wait.

Kristen enjoyed the novel position of being able to look down on him. All that rich, dark hair, just waiting for her to mess up—and if she sat at just the right angle, she could see a bit of his chest below the unbuttoned V at his throat. He had no farmer's tan, just more yummy bronzed skin...

He looked up at her, catching her staring.

She was so busted, but she didn't bite her lip or blush or look away. She'd learned a long time ago to brazen out embarrassing situations.

"You were sitting right here when I first saw you," he said.

If he'd seen her sitting on the fence, then he'd seen

her before the carriage had arrived. She hadn't spotted him first, after all.

Why didn't you approach me right away? That was too bold even for her. She tried a different question. "What did you think about the girl on the fence?"

"That you were happy. You were laughing with your sister. I envied you."

"For having a sister?" She shook her head and answered her own question. "No, you have a sister of your own. You envied us for laughing. Are you not happy?"

"Is that a trick question? Do you mean for the next five minutes, or do you mean my life in general?"

She smiled at his light words, but her curiosity grew. "Let's start with at the moment."

He didn't answer her immediately, looking away to gaze calmly at the horizon and the first streaks of the sunset appearing over the mountain peaks.

She thunked her heels on the railing, stopped herself and smoothed her skirt over her knees. She'd rather be smoothing his dark hair.

"I met a wonderful woman today," he said, "and she's tolerating my company without complaint. I'm happy."

"Good answer, but that was a mighty long pause." She wanted to see his face, so she climbed down and leaned against the fence beside him, watching his profile as he watched the horizon. "I thought 'Are you happy?' would be an easy yes or no."

"I don't usually think in terms of being happy. It sounds frivolous."

She slipped her hand in his. It felt familiar, for they'd been holding hands in the traditional ballroom holds that went with the waltz and the two-step, but it also felt significant. There was no excuse of a dance this time.

He rubbed his thumb along the back of her hand, as if they often held hands while they talked.

"It's not frivolous, though," he said. "Happiness is serious. It's the driving force behind our lives. 'The pursuit of happiness' is a legal right. We all have the right to try to find it."

"To try." She echoed the words he'd emphasized. "Have you been successful in your attempt?"

He raised their joined hands and placed a light kiss on her knuckle.

"Today, yes."

She made him happy.

She sucked in a little breath at the compliment. But he'd said *today*, as if happiness were a rare occurrence.

"Isn't your life usually happy?"

"I'm working on it," he said with all the confidence of a man who was certain he'd solve a problem soon.

That kind of confidence must be nice to have. "How do you work on happiness?"

"My job isn't as fulfilling as it once was. I need to reevaluate. Refocus."

Kristen could imagine that even if he was born for the rodeo, it could easily be more stressful than happy. Rodeo careers were physically punishing and therefore short. He looked to be about thirty. He'd said he was considering a change of pace, getting out of the fast lane, but maybe he was being forced to by circumstances.

"It's more than my career, though. I find myself envying my brother and sister." He paused, and Kristen suspected that he was giving these thoughts voice for the first time. "Within a year of each other, they got married. My sister had a baby just a few months ago, and my brother is expecting his first."

"So now they're happy?"

"I wouldn't have said they were unhappy people before. They had great careers and a family they could rely on, but I can see that they have more now. Even though they weren't missing anything, they found something else, anyway, and now they are really living. Or more accurately, I should say they found some*one* else. Not a thing, a person."

A little distance away, the bride laughingly yelped as she and Braden were pelted with birdseed as they ran toward the opening in the fence. The groom's black truck was parked on the street beyond.

Ryan didn't move as the whole wedding party came closer. "I'm starting to believe it's not how much fame and fortune you have, but whether or not you have someone by your side."

As Braden and his bride ran past them, Kristen waved and shouted "good luck," but they already seemed incredibly lucky to her. She and her sister had started the afternoon by wishing they had what the newlyweds had. It hadn't occurred to Kristen that she ought to do something about it besides hope and wait. Ryan was right about pursuing happiness. It was sobering to realize that she'd been so passive about her life.

"I'm sorry," Ryan said quietly, and she realized he was studying her closely. "Here we are at a happy occasion, and I'm being too maudlin and reflective. Montana has that effect on me."

"Montana makes you sad?"

"Montana makes me think. I wish I didn't have to

leave tomorrow. I feel more at peace here than anywhere else."

Then he'd be coming back.

She felt her buoyant mood returning. The truth was,
no matter how much she admired Ryan's determination,
hoping and wishing had worked for Kristen. Who was
she to double-guess how the universe worked?

The groom opened the passenger door of his truck
and began helping his bride gather up her full skirts so
she could climb in. He knew which door to open for her
because his friends had very helpfully used white shoe
polish on the window to write the words *Bride Goes
Here* with an arrow.

Kristen gave Ryan a gentle nudge with her shoulder.
"The truck isn't as romantic as the carriage, but infi-
nitely more practical. It wouldn't be too romantic to
ride off into the sunset and then spend the first hours
of your wedding night unhitching a team and stabling
the horses, would it?"

"I would never argue with a cowgirl. If you say unhitching horses would delay the fireworks, then I trust
you."

"You're just humoring me now." He was doing that
serious-joking thing again, implying she knew more
about horses than he did.

"I'd bet the ranch that you live on a ranch. You must
know horses."

The black truck drove off, the cluster of empty cans
that were tied to its tailpipe clattering loudly behind it.
Ryan gave their joined hands a tug and started leading
her along the fence, away from the send-off crowd who
were now milling about.

"I do live on a ranch, but what made you guess that?

Do I smell like I mucked the stables this morning? I'm not saying I did, but is there hay in my hair? Or do I just snicker like a horse when I laugh?"

He stopped walking once they reached a cluster of spruce trees. She moved a little closer into his personal space.

He didn't back up an inch. This close, in order for him to look down at her, his eyes got that heavy-lidded look. Bedroom eyes.

"Those aren't the clues that you live on a ranch."

"The boots, then?" She felt a little nervous, a little excited. Ryan had been willing to follow her playful lead all day, but the way he looked at her now left no doubt that he was a man who knew where the game was leading—and who'd know exactly what to do when they got there.

"You must be a cowgirl because you have incredible stamina," he murmured, "on the dance floor."

A shiver threatened to run down her spine.

"You practically glow with health. Your hair, your skin. You. Every single inch of you." They were so very close, bodies nearly touching in the quiet twilight, the sounds of the band and the crowd far in the background.

She wanted to kiss him. She could go up on tiptoe and taste his lips as she'd been dying to do forever, but she wanted him to initiate it. Good girls didn't steal the first kiss. How such an old-fashioned notion had been ingrained in her brain was beyond her, but there it was. She kept holding his hand, wanting so much more.

An evening breeze carried the crisp air from the distant mountains into the park, stirring the evergreen sent of the spruce trees, blowing a few strands of her loose hair over her cheeks. Ryan brushed them back, those bedroom eyes making the touch of his hand on her hair as sensual a feeling as she'd ever experienced.

As Ryan tamed her hair, she stayed still, wishing, wishing. His body was so much larger than hers, his muscles moving under the polished cotton of his shirt with the gentle motion of his hand.

Kiss me.

He let the last lock of her hair go, and his fingers brushed the bare skin of her shoulders, then higher, a smooth, light run up the length of her neck, a barely there brush of fingertips on her jaw.

Kiss me, kiss me.

The gentle touch of his fingertips was replaced by the sure warmth of his palm as he cupped her face in his hand. Her eyes closed.

Kiss me.

"Kristen Dalton." When he spoke her name, she felt the whisper of his breath on her lips. "Where have you been all my life?"

"Right here, waiting for you to find some happiness."

He kissed her, and, oh, it was a glorious feeling of soft lips and restraint, a tender you-may-kiss-the-bride moment. He ended it too soon, and she opened her eyes. Behind him, the sunset had come into its full colors over the snow-capped mountains that had defined the horizon her entire life.

Had she expected the kiss to make him happy? He wasn't smiling. His gaze was direct, his face so serious it was almost a frown.

Before she could say something, anything at all, he let go of her hand to hold her face between both of his palms. Words fled. He pulled her to him for a kiss that rocked her world. Rougher, more greedy. Possessive, more passionate.

Her fingers slid into the hair at the nape of his neck as he pulled her into him more tightly than any dance had allowed. She felt the hard planes of his body, and everything soft in her wanted to give in and melt in the safety of his arms.

She kissed him until his arms felt more sexy than safe. She kissed him until the only reason she was standing was that he held her up.

If he could have laid her down, if they hadn't been hiding in plain sight in a corner of the town park, she would have gone willingly. It would be madness, but finally, she understood the crazy things couples did. Love at first sight, undeniable desire, life-changing decisions made in a split second—it all made perfect sense.

He ended the kiss when she would not have, could not have. As they held tightly to each other, she could feel every breath that filled his chest. She panted softly herself, as if she'd run a mile. Run a mile, and won the race. The endorphin rush, the thrill of knowing that *this* had happened, that she'd found the one man with whom she connected more strongly than she'd known was possible, was almost frightening.

He placed gentle kisses on her temple and at the corner of her eye, little echoes of the passion that had just obliterated all her thoughts. "You smell fantastic, by the way."

It took her a second to remember what they'd been talking about before the kiss. "Not like a stable?"

"Like summer."

"Your favorite."

And then they were kissing again, hungry and intense. She wanted him with a desperation that threatened once more to make her shameless. He broke off the kiss but clutched her closer. His breath was harsh in her ear. "That was damned…"

"Scary?" she whispered.

"Powerful."

She pulled back a little bit. All the emotions overwhelming her were reflected in his expression, too. It made her feel even closer to him, to the one person who was weathering this unpredictable storm with her.

"I think…" She didn't have any clear thoughts, only feelings. Crazy, uninhibited feelings today, here in the town park. She looked up at him through her lashes, hoping to lighten the intensity. "I think we just found a great way to pursue happiness."

His smile was brief. "I still have to leave tomorrow. The fact that I'm falling for the most beautiful girl in the world doesn't change the fact that I have people depending on me."

Falling for her. He was falling for her, and everything was right in the world—except that he had to leave tomorrow. She didn't like it, but she understood it. The rodeo wasn't so different from the theater in many ways.

"The show must go on," she said.

"And on, and on. I get to enjoy the victories for about five seconds before the next challenge begins. But we still have tonight. How would you like to spend it?"

He had to ask?

She kissed him this time. He responded instantly, perfectly, opening his mouth to her demands, anchoring her to him with his hands. He kept the kiss from exploding into desperation this time, setting a slower pace, a more luxurious exploration. It was divine to kiss him, the sensation so perfect that it was like seeing a new color she'd never known existed or hearing a beautiful piece of music for the first time.

He broke off the kiss with a softly spoken *damn*.

"Ryan," she begged.

"I know." He tucked her securely against his chest. She breathed in the warm skin exposed at his throat. "I know."

Where are you staying? Let's leave the park now. The words wouldn't come, too many years of that good-girl upbringing preventing her from saying what she wanted.

"I have to leave tomorrow," he said, so quietly that she wondered if he was speaking to himself. "It would be...we should just...we shouldn't."

There was nothing else to say. A part of her wanted to plead childishly, *Don't you want to?* Or more importantly, *Don't you want me?*

She stayed silent, her cheek to his chest. He was older than she was and almost certainly more experienced, but she trusted herself to answer those questions. Yes, he wanted to. Yes, he wanted *her*. She could feel the muscle tension in his body. He was deliberately keeping himself under control. His breathing was steady only because he was requiring himself to breathe steadily.

He was being a true cowboy, one with all the courtesy and respect that a gentleman traditionally showed a lady. Hadn't she vowed she'd settle for nothing less?

Frankly, she wished the universe hadn't listened to her quite so thoroughly on that point. This man was hers, and they would be together sooner or later, and her body was certainly eager for sooner. With a sigh, she lifted her head and stepped back just a tiny bit, keeping her arms looped around his waist.

"I guess it's too early for fireworks," she said.

The corner of his mouth quirked in that hint of amusement she was coming to love. When the breeze blew her hair forward again, she tried to toss it back with a shake of her head, refusing to let go of Ryan.

He pushed her hair back for her and kept his hands on either side of her face. "I can hardly believe you're real."

"Wanna kiss me again to be sure?"

He laughed at that, a much needed break in the tension. "I know you're real. Amazingly, incredibly real. But today hasn't been. This isn't my real life." He let go of her face.

"But it could be. That's what you came here to decide."

He stepped back, and she let him go. Desire that could not be satisfied wasn't a desirable state to be in. But then he turned away from her—and from the sunset, the mountains, everything. He braced his hands on the fence and looked down at the railing.

As if the man hadn't already stirred up enough emotions in her, she now felt the tender tug of sympathy. There was some pain in the way he bowed his head as well as strength in the set of his jaw. It must be hard for a man's career to be ending when most people were just hitting their strides. The rodeo was unforgiving, and Ryan seemed determined to choose his next step in a purely objective manner. But any man who knew horses and victory and defeat, any man who appreciated music and summer and family, must have a heart.

She hoped he'd listen to his.

"Should I leave my current life and start a new one in

Rust Creek Falls? That's the essential question. I can't drop the commitments I've already made. Being impulsive would hurt too many people. Today was supposed to just be a first step. I only came to see the town and begin evaluating my options."

"That's perfectly logical." She said it with a straight face, the way he had over dinner.

He glanced sideways at her. "You don't think so?"

"I think you've already made up your mind. All this ponderous decision-making isn't necessary, but if it makes you feel better, ponder away."

Her attempts at humor were helping her regain some equilibrium, anyway. She turned around to lean back on the fence, resting her elbows on the top rail and hitching the heel of one boot on the bottom. She let her head drop back far enough so she could look up at the darkening sky.

She managed at least sixty seconds of silence before peeking at Ryan. He'd stopped brooding at the fence, at least, and was watching her. She supposed she bore some resemblance to the ranch dogs who flopped onto their backs when they wanted a belly rub.

"It would have been easier if I'd never kissed you." Judging from the deep bass in his voice, maybe she looked better than she thought.

"Then I'm glad you kissed me."

"Kristen Dalton, you are a serious complication."

"Nope." She pushed off the fence and mirrored his stance, arms crossed over her chest, standing solidly on her own two cowboy-booted feet. "I'm just a big, positive check mark on your balance sheet. You're determined to decide your next step very methodically, I can tell. When you make your official list of pluses and minuses, you'll put me on the plus side in bold letters."

"Kristen."

She waited as he tried to think of the right thing to say, but apparently she'd said something so logical, he couldn't refute it. It was almost as good as making him forget to hold the horse earlier in the day.

"In the meantime, we could stay here, alone, practically invisible to everyone else once darkness falls. Fireworks of one kind or another are bound to happen. That would surely go in the plus column."

He acted like he was giving the idea serious consideration. "Being arrested for public indecency would give me a chance to see the local jail cells firsthand. A well-run police force would go in the plus column."

"I'm sure the cells are lovely, but someone would have to catch us in the act first, and these spruce trees are mighty hard to see through. Did you notice they smell like Christmas?"

"Now that you mention it." He seemed faintly surprised at her words.

"It's the perfect blend for us, summer and Christmas."

Ryan moved to escort her out of their little corner of the world. "I think we need to keep ourselves busy while we wait for the fireworks. Should we head back to the dance floor?"

"You came here to see Rust Creek Falls. I just so happen to have known this town for twenty-five years. I'll give you a tour. You can rack up more check marks in the plus column."

Kristen pointed toward the gate that the bride and groom had used to leave on their honeymoon. "The first step is right this way. You're going to love everything you see."

She glanced up at him just as he said, "I think I already do."

He'd been looking at her, not at the town, when he'd said it.

If she could have blown a kiss to the universe, she would have.

Chapter Four

Ryan was losing his mind—but at least he was losing it while having one of the greatest days of his life with the most enchanting woman he'd ever met. He enjoyed every moment in Kristen's company, every teasing comment, every exuberant laugh, every country-western dance.

But that kiss had been a whole different world. The first taste of her mouth had rocketed into an intense need to make her his, desire going from zero to sixty in one second. It had been primal, almost frightening in its intensity. He was thirty-three years old, yet a kiss, a single kiss while fully clothed, had him rethinking everything he thought he knew about craving a woman's touch.

One particular woman's touch. Kristen Dalton, who somewhere between a waltz and a two-step had made a better life seem possible.

Kristen stopped outside the park and waited for one

lone pickup truck to pass them, then led him across the street. As they walked, he put his arm around her shoulders, left so thankfully bare by her summer dress. She slid her arm around his waist, a move as natural as if they'd been lovers forever. There was a rightness to it.

A rightness? There was that fate nonsense again. When had he ever thought or felt or wondered about the rightness of a casual touch?

Give up the analysis. Just enjoy the rest of the day.

"First stop on your tour. The local junior-senior high school. Go Grizzlies." She beamed at the brick structure, a plain two-story rectangle, government architecture at its most common.

"*The* school? There's only one?"

"There's an elementary school, but this is the one and only high school. It's very important to Rust Creek Falls. Whether you're a teenager or not, this is the hot place to be on a Friday night. It's our number one cure for cabin fever in the winter. When you can't stand seeing solid white out your window, come to the gym for the varsity basketball game. The whole town will be here, not to mention everyone from the opposing team's town. The clash of school colors will dazzle you after months of snow. There's pop and soft pretzels, and you can cheer the players and boo the referee. It'll get you through until spring."

He pretended to consider the building seriously. "It sounds like an item for the minus column. Solid white out your window that gives you cabin fever? Not so great."

"The snow isn't the town's fault, so you can't ding us for that. But to provide a cure for cabin fever?" She spread her hands out to encompass the school. "Definite plus."

It was ludicrous to think that he, Ryan Roarke, with his courtside seats at NBA playoffs, would count it as a *definite plus* to sit on gym bleachers and watch adolescents attempt to shoot hoops. He was accustomed to watching the best athletes in the world. He expected to be entertained by world-class professional cheerleaders. He knew how—

Professional cheerleader. He'd completely forgotten the Laker Girl he'd so recently left. She hadn't entered his thoughts for more than a moment after they'd parted ways, although they'd dated on and off for some time. And yet, had his sister not mentioned this town-wide wedding celebration, he would probably have been with that cheerleader right now, and she with him, simply for the convenience of having an appropriate "plus one" for a yachting weekend that was more about business than relaxation.

He knew other men envied him for never lacking in female companionship, but today—this crazy, emotional day—it seemed more pathetic than prestigious to waste time with a woman who meant nothing to him.

He looked down at Kristen. She was gesturing toward the distant baseball diamond as she told him about more school sporting events, her face radiant even as darkness settled around them. It had been easy for him to come to Montana and forget about a woman in LA, but Ryan knew he'd find it impossible to forget about Kristen when he left Montana. If he could take with him some of her zest for life, he would.

"You must have enjoyed being a student here. Or was it a torturous teenage experience?"

"Ah, another trick question. I want you to think I'm cool, so I should say high school was cool. But I don't want you to think I was too cool, so I should make sure you know I had my moments of angst. Honestly, I was always afraid I didn't fit in."

"You? Not fit in?" The idea was laughable.

"I was pretty insecure at sixteen, but I guess that's normal. Isn't it?"

Something in her voice, a trace of that insecurity, made him look at her more closely.

"Didn't you worry if you fit in?" she persisted.

He had, but it had been assumed by the adults in his life that it was a consequence of his early childhood. He'd been particularly withdrawn his sophomore year, and he'd overheard his parents debating whether or not they should take him to a psychologist. They'd wondered if it was normal teenage angst, as Kristen called it, or damage from being abandoned by his birth mother.

They'd concluded it was just a normal phase, but as he'd eavesdropped on their conversation, he'd concluded the opposite. He could remember the hem of his mother's dress as she'd walked away. No one else had a memory like that. Not his brother, not his sister, not his parents. There had to be something horribly wrong with him.

Thankfully, Kristen had never known that kind of pain. She'd introduced him to her twin on the dance floor. She'd waved at a man she'd told him was one of her brothers, although Ryan had already guessed as much from their resemblance. Kristen had been born into a close family, not adopted after being left behind. She'd been raised with love from the first day of her life.

It was incredible to hear her say that she'd worried

about fitting in. Kristen was outgoing and friendly in a natural way. She had to be welcome everywhere she went. If a woman like Kristen had spent her high school years wondering if she belonged, then maybe his parents had been right. Maybe his teenage years hadn't been anything out of the ordinary.

Kristen was looking up at him, patiently waiting for his answer.

"I worried, too."

But maybe that was normal. It was a radical thought.

She gave him a squeeze. "I told you we had so much in common."

He said nothing, thrown off-kilter by yet another loop on the day's emotional roller coaster, but then Kristen rested her head on his shoulder, and everything seemed to right itself again.

"I've been trying to get some after-school activities going here. The principal said the budget wouldn't allow for another student club. Maybe next semester. Always next semester. Anyway, are you ready for the next stop on your tour? There's a really great donut shop on the next block. It might be worth two pluses."

A teacher. Kristen didn't just live on a ranch and care for horses; she was a teacher. She spoke as if he'd already known it, but he'd missed it somehow—probably while he'd been tracing her curves, gliding his palms over the material of her dress.

He wanted to know more about her. He wasn't so blinded by lust that he'd overlooked her as a person. In fact, every detail about her out of bed contributed to how strongly he wanted her *in* his bed—but currently, his bed was in Los Angeles. Whether or not it should stay there was the question this little tour was supposed to help answer.

Kristen was more interesting to him than the town. He sat on the base of the high school sign and made room for her to sit with him. "What are you going to do if the principal puts you off until 'next semester' again?"

"I'll keep doing what I'm doing. There's always plenty of work at the ranch." She straightened out one leg and studied the toe of her boot. "The last time I interviewed with him, I hit the feed store on the way home. I remember thinking how odd it was to wear my nice professional pumps and carry chicken feed."

"It must be frustrating to have gotten that college degree and then not use it."

It was the wrong thing to say. Kristen stared at him, her blue eyes wide, and then she seemed to crumple a little, sagging against the school sign. "I hadn't thought of it that way. I just thought it would be good to have something to do outside of the ranch. Kayla does some copyediting for the local paper. I kind of envy her for having a little desk in an office in town. But wasting my degree? That sounds terrible."

Ryan wished he could take the words back. As an attorney, he knew that was impossible. They were out there now, on the record. For Kristen, though, he had to try.

"Forget I said that. You belong on that family ranch. You're lucky to be part of something like that."

"No, you made a good point. If I'm not going to use my degree, why did I bother getting it?"

"Pursuing an education is never a waste."

She wrinkled her nose.

He tried again. "Education is its own reward."

His irrepressible Kristen started to smile. "You're trying to make me feel better, aren't you?"

"I truly don't think it's a waste to have gotten an education." As always, her smile was infectious. He felt a little sheepish, but he smiled back. "And yes, I really wish I hadn't said that. I didn't mean to make you sad."

"No apology necessary. You said Montana didn't make you sad, it made you think. You're just making me think."

"And that's a good thing?"

"It's good, but it's not the best thing. The best thing is when you're making it impossible for me to think at all."

With a swish of denim, she stood and turned and then nestled on his lap. Everything he wanted in the world was suddenly in his arms, and it was all Kristen. The weight of her body, the feel of her skin, the smell of her hair and the taste of her mouth overwhelmed his senses. All his worries about normalcy were obliterated. This passion was far outside the boring bounds of normalcy, because the woman in his arms was extraordinary.

Ryan never wanted normal again.

Kristen continued the town tour under strict orders: no kissing.

She and Ryan couldn't seem to master a simple kiss. Outside the school, she'd wanted to be playful when she'd sat in his lap, but once the kissing started, it had gotten serious, fast.

Again.

Hard sidewalks had a way of imposing a limit on how far even consenting adults could go, however, so they'd eventually resumed their little tour, holding hands as they headed up the next street toward Daisy's Donuts.

"This building is one of the oldest ones, built in 1889. The rest of the brick ones on this side of the street are from the years the railroad was built. My mom remembers when this building was a five and dime, but now it's a boring old dentist office. It was built in 1909."

"Did they make you memorize this in school, or do you just have a good memory for that sort of thing?"

An unladylike snort of laughter escaped her. She'd been pulling the wool over Ryan's eyes for a full block of Victorian buildings.

"The only reason I know how old these buildings are is because almost all of them have the year they were built carved in stone. Look up there, at the very top of that building. It must have been a common thing to chisel the year into the keystone or the crenellation or whatever that's called."

"Trickery. Devious residents in this town. I think that has to go in the minus column."

"It's not a minus that a Rust Creek Falls native can read a date that is written in stone. If anything, it proves that the town has intelligent residents."

She stopped in front of the donut shop and faced Ryan. "They serve coffee and bear claws here that count as a plus. They get points for being extra cute, too. Bear claws in the home of the Grizzlies. Bears. Grizzlies. Why aren't you laughing?"

"Do we have any minuses yet? One?"

She stepped closer and wrapped her arms around his waist. "Considering how I want you to come back the first possible moment you can, it's not in my best interest to point out any downsides. You're looking pretty serious. Are you thinking of something negative?"

"Not when I'm looking at you."

She didn't know whether to melt into a puddle or squeeze him fiercely at those words. Her body kind of shivered in a mixture of the two. He broke his own rule with a swift kiss, then resumed their walk.

They didn't have far to go. Now that Kristen saw it through his eyes, the town really was small. At the end of the street, she turned to walk a block along the river that had overflowed its banks two years ago. Tonight, the river was as tame and steady as it had been most of her life. The town might be really small, but it was really perfect.

Kristen tried to imagine what was missing, what kind of thing would count as a minus when Ryan went through the pros and cons to make the decision she was certain his heart had already made.

When she'd moved away, finances had been in her minus column in New York. Ryan wasn't a broke college student, however. He must do very well on the rodeo circuit. His boots and belt were very fine leather. Even the buttons of his shirt were a quality she'd never seen on the shirts her father ordered from the Sears catalog.

Her father had missed her while she'd been at college, of course, and she'd missed him. Maybe family was an issue for Ryan.

"Would moving to Rust Creek Falls bring you closer to your parents, or farther away?"

He slowed his steps. "Much farther away, and you read my mind."

"Missing your parents would be a big minus, then. Will they be surprised if you choose Rust Creek Falls when you settle down?"

"Shocked, but if I decide to do this, they'll support

me. They've always been very goal-oriented people, but their main goal has always been to see their kids happy."

"Even if the pursuit of happiness leads away from home?"

"My brother and sister have already put them through that test. My brother most of all, when he decided to look for his birth mother. If that was what his pursuit of happiness required, then my parents supported him one hundred percent."

"Are you adopted, too?"

"All three of us, each adopted separately. We're not genetically siblings. Closed adoptions. It was a challenge for my brother to locate his birth family."

She felt her lips quirk in a Ryan-like half smile. "You sound like me, giving the answers to the frequently asked questions before anyone asks them. Mine goes, 'We're identical, not fraternal, there were no fertility drugs involved and twins do not run in the family.' Oh—and, 'Yes, I do believe my parents were surprised. Wouldn't you be?'"

He chuckled. "Should I admit that I didn't realize you were identical? In my defense, we only danced past your sister a few times. You are so uniquely you, though. I can't imagine mistaking you for anyone else. Does it happen a lot?"

"Sure. My parents have never been fooled, though."

"Parents are like that."

Kristen swung their hands a little and looked up at the stars. It was fully night and a little chilly, but she felt so content with the world at the moment she didn't mind a thing. "So, your brother found his birth family. Have you looked for your birth mother?"

"No." He rubbed his jaw, and she wondered if it still

hurt where the horse had hit him. "That is—no. I've got no need to."

Why not? The question was on the tip of her tongue, but his *no* had been so curt, she hesitated.

As the breeze from the river teased the ends of her hair, he frowned a bit. "The temperature has dropped. You must be freezing."

Despite the warm day, it usually dropped into the fifties at night, and she was in a halter dress that left a lot of her upper half bare. She'd jumped into her brother's truck to come to the wedding reception, and that was where she'd left her jacket and her phone, darn it.

"I'll be fine." Just to make her out as a liar, her body betrayed her by shivering. "You could put your arm around me."

He did, and they continued along the river, but he was silent and a little edgy beside her.

"This is Main Street." She wanted to lighten up the mood of their little tour. "It's one-stop shopping here for all your municipal needs."

"You've got goose bumps." He let go of her and started unbuttoning his shirt.

"Are you *literally* going to give me the shirt off your back? You can't walk around here undressed. I mean, I've never actually looked up the public indecency laws, but that can't be right. Not that the women of this town would mind a bunch of shirtless cowboys wandering around, but—"

"I'm *literally* wearing two shirts, and you've got none."

Sure enough, when he took off his dress shirt, he had a T-shirt on underneath. A tight, white, body-hugging T-shirt, tucked into his jeans. Good heavens, the universe was pulling out all the stops.

"Ryan…"

When she reached for him, he started dressing her in his shirt, tugging a sleeve over her outstretched hand. His moves were efficient, but it was undeniably sensual to feel his warm shirt on her arms and feel the tickle of his shirt collar on the back of her neck.

"Better?" he asked.

"Thanks." She pulled her long hair free from the collar as he tied the shirttails in a knot at her waist.

His hands lingered for a moment, before he put them on his own hips and squarely faced her. It occurred to her that he could hook his thumbs in his belt loops and yank off a pair of tear-away pants just like that. Not that she'd seen too many male stripper movies.

"I didn't mean to be so curt about my adoption. I'm not curious about my birth mother the way my brother was about his, because I remember her."

In a flash, all the sexual thoughts she'd been entertaining were banked, and concern for him took center stage.

"He was adopted as an infant, but I was almost four. That's still too young to remember much, but what I remember is… It's enough."

And it was enough to make him withdraw from her. The change was subtle, but his stance was tight, controlled. Like he was braced for a fight.

"Did she hurt you?" The idea of Ryan being abused as a toddler was enough to make her sick. All the wedding punch and picnic food churned in her stomach.

It must have showed on her face, because he took her hand again, his grip strong as he threaded his fingers through hers. "As far as anyone could tell, I hadn't been battered in any way. I've been told I was a little underweight, but not significantly malnourished."

"Well, that's good." Such weak words, but she didn't know what else to say. The child he'd been had to be an important part of the man he'd become, but she couldn't pepper him with questions, not like she had over dinner. Not on this topic.

Somewhere on a pop psychology blog, she'd read that men were more comfortable talking when they had something physical to do, so rather than stare at the dark river, she started walking. They turned onto Main Street, silently, together.

Kristen caught her breath at the scene. The street was completely deserted, not one car parked on the edge of the road. The streetlights were soft yellow globes, evenly spaced, drawing the eye down the dark road. The buildings flanked them on either side, standing like timeless brick sentinels in long rows that disappeared into the darkness a few blocks away. Beyond them, the snowcapped mountains marked the horizon, their white peaks lit by the full moon.

"I've never seen it like this," she whispered into the night. "It's like we're the only two people in the entire town. Just you and me."

They left the sidewalk to walk down the center of the deserted street. He must have felt the magic, too. They were the only two people in the world, safe and intimate in the open air. Where better to confide secrets?

As they walked, Ryan began to do just that. "She left me standing on the steps of a church."

"Do you remember her face?"

"I remember the backs of her legs. I remember the hem of her dress as she walked away. She was irritated with me, but I still wanted to follow her. I didn't have anyone else to belong to. The only person I knew in the whole world was walking away."

Kristen held tightly to his hand. He was so tall and athletic, her cowboy, confident, too. It should have been hard to imagine him as a vulnerable preschooler, but the look in his eyes as he remembered that moment touched her heart.

"I'm so sorry. That's a terrible memory."

"It's a useful memory. Without it, I would probably be like my brother, wondering if I had a birth parent out there, and wondering if they would be glad or horrified to hear from me. It's not easy to decide to start that search. In my case, I don't have to go through that. I already know. She didn't want me. She wasn't being noble and giving an accidental baby a chance at a better life. She wasn't torn up inside because she couldn't provide for a child. She just ditched me without any tenderness. Knowing that has saved me from wasting my time and money searching for a woman who wouldn't be glad to hear from me."

Kristen was afraid she'd sob if she spoke, if she could have even thought of something appropriate to say, which she couldn't. She also couldn't stand that remote coolness in his voice. She had to do something.

So she hugged him. She simply wrapped her arms around him and rested her cheek on his chest and hugged him.

His arms came around her immediately, reassuringly. "It's okay, Kristen. It was thirty years ago. Are you crying?"

"Only a little." She sniffed in hard to stop the tears,

determined not to soak the cotton of his T-shirt. "Tell me that your adoptive parents were wonderful."

"My parents were wonderful. They are wonderful still. Why?"

"I just want your story to have a happy ending."

She didn't think he'd found it yet. Then again, they hadn't met before today. She hugged him harder, hoping he could see how much better their lives would be when they could pursue happiness together.

Ryan tried to get his emotions under control. Why in the hell had he shared the worst memory of his life?

He'd come here to see Maggie's new baby. That should have been enough for this trip far from Los Angeles. A pleasant wedding, a Montana-style wedding toast from a paper cup, and he should have been on his way.

Instead, Kristen had waltzed into his arms, and now he never wanted to leave.

He had to. If he didn't fly out tomorrow, a struggling screenwriter whose day in court had come would surely lose his challenge. His material had been stolen by a powerful studio. The man's life's work could go unrecognized and unrecompensed. Ryan was trying to stop a robbery in progress—and that was just Monday's case.

Los Angeles was his life. Today was just pretend, but Kristen's arms wrapped around him were real. Her tears were, too, and he'd unintentionally caused them. He never spoke about his birth mother. He shouldn't have started now. He and Kristen had precious little time left, and he didn't want to spend it making a lovely woman sad.

Her tour had been charming, her list of positive check marks all hopelessly naive and yet there was an undeniable truth that school spirit and homemade pastries were two of life's joys. He wanted the tour to continue.

I want her to show me something that will make me come back to stay. For real.

How could he possibly justify this move? Telling Kristen about his abandonment hadn't helped. It had only reinforced how much he owed to his parents. If he couldn't leave Roarke and Associates because clients needed him, then he absolutely couldn't leave the Roarkes themselves after all they'd done for him.

Convince me anyway, Kristen.

He ran his palm over her hair. She relaxed her grip and looked up at him, her blue eyes bright with unshed tears, her smile outshining them with her effervescent spirit.

Ryan lost his heart.

He wanted to believe something could come of it.

"Let's finish this tour. You were telling me about the wonders of Main Street." He turned to walk toward that faraway white-capped mountain, leaving the last Victorian facades as the buildings became more modern, with spacious stretches of grass between them. "I don't see a year on the keystone of this one. In fact, I don't see a keystone."

"The library. Built in, um…"

"No trickery."

"Well, I went to story hours there as a little girl, so I can guesstimate that the building is roughly twenty-five years old." She gestured to the other side of the street. "I know this one exactly. The community center is brand-spanking-new, built after the flood. The funds came in from an anonymous donor."

Ryan didn't stop her monologue, but he knew all

about the Grace Traub Community Center. Shane's birth father had contributed the money in honor of Shane's deceased birth mother.

"They built it in the perfect spot," she said, drawing him back onto the sidewalk as they continued past the community center. She stopped to point out the two-story town hall across the street, telling him about the monthly town meetings and how accessible he'd find the mayor when he moved here.

Looming at their backs was the church where the day's wedding had taken place, a traditional structure with a steeple that reached for the night stars. Wide, white steps led from the arched double doors down to the sidewalk. He ignored them.

"Living in a town this size is efficient. I'll give you the classic example, one every good Rust Creek Falls resident makes use of eventually, even though we all joke about it. You get your marriage license at the city hall." Kristen turned to look up at the church. "You walk across the street to the church and make your promises in front of the preacher, and then you head to the community center to cut your cake and have your first dance."

A bridal couple would have to pass the exact spot where they stood. Ryan had parked behind the church this afternoon and had entered through a side door. It hadn't been an intentional move to avoid church steps. He never did that—they were only concrete, after all. Tonight, they looked ominous, a ridiculous trick of the mind after an emotional day.

Kristen started up the steps ahead of him, taking them briskly, talking cheerfully. "Having the reception at the Fourth of July celebration today was a real departure from tradition."

It had been cold the day his mother left him. The church had been having some kind of Christmas festival, and he'd been given one of those cheap plastic snow globes. He could remember the hard feel of it in his hands as he'd watched his mother walk away.

"I've never seen a patriotic wedding like today's. The red, white and blue thing worked out great, didn't you think?"

Ryan put his boot on the first step and he saw, in his mind's eye, a shattered snow globe. He'd dropped the snow globe after his mother left. He'd forgotten that. For thirty years, he'd forgotten that, until now.

He saw the splattered water darkening the white steps. The shards of plastic. The bits of glitter that weren't as magical when they weren't clustered together. He didn't remember being sad in that moment, only resigned. He'd known before his fourth birthday that nothing good lasted very long.

Kristen's voice came down softly from above him. "Ah, church steps."

Her intuition was amazing to him. From the first moment they'd danced together, she'd been able to read the most subtle change in him.

She came down to the sidewalk. When he kept staring at his boot on the step, she slipped her hand into the bend of his elbow, as if he were escorting her to a formal affair. "Maybe if a man stood on a set of church steps with his bride beside him, it would give him a better memory to wipe that old one away."

She set her foot next to his, the fancy leather scrollwork of her boot obliterating the vision of the shattered snow globe. She was a bold one, this delicate-looking beauty raised in the land of glaciers and grizzlies.

"Maybe it would," he said quietly. "Maybe the ghost of young Ryan Michaels would finally disappear."

He wanted to believe so. Everything good didn't have to end. He'd just handled too many divorces and worked with too many people who were on their third and fourth marriages. In Rust Creek Falls, it seemed possible that two people could stick to one promise. Something good could last.

"I think young Ryan Michaels turned into a good man," Kristen said softly.

He lifted Kristen's hand to press a kiss in her palm. Everything seemed possible today, that the child Ryan Michaels and the man Ryan Roarke weren't so completely separate. That he, Ryan, could even meet the one perfect woman for him.

Kristen climbed the step to stand face-to-face with him. She rested her forehead against his, and he closed his eyes.

"Maybe," she said, "a man and a woman could decide to skip the church steps altogether. They could get their license and say their vows, too, in the town hall."

"But that's not how it's usually done in this town. If the bride had grown up here, she might feel like she missed out on her big day." *If she tied herself down to a man no one knew, a man who was a stranger to the local norms.* "People would talk."

"People would wonder why, but if it made the grown-up version of Ryan Michaels happier not to think about church steps at all, then she'd be happier if she could skip that part, too. They're promising to be a team from that day forward, and if it would make a less stressful wedding day for them as a team, that would be all that mattered."

"Kristen." He hadn't been looking for her; he hadn't thought a woman would ever understand him so well. Yet she'd been here in this tiny town in Montana, and he'd known, somehow, to come and find her today.

Fate. Destiny. Magic. He was ready to believe all of it.

He picked her up off the step and whirled her into the street. She landed lightly on her feet, laughing with him, gesturing toward the Traub Community Center. "Of course, they'd still have a grand reception. Everyone would come, but it would be just the two of them alone on the dance floor for their first dance."

"It wouldn't be a first dance for us." Ryan took her into his arms to waltz once more. In the middle of the street in their own private town, he led her in the elegant steps of the ballroom dance, thighs brushing in the dark as she hummed a country-western tune.

The fireworks were inevitable. The park was only two blocks away, so the fireworks were spectacularly close, their umbrella shapes forming shimmering willow trees over Ryan and Kristen as they continued to waltz, turning around and around on the solid yellow traffic lines that crossed the dark pavement under their boots.

It was just as inevitable that the fireworks would end, their last burst of thunder echoing off the buildings around them. Ryan and Kristen stopped, slightly out of breath from their dance, slightly breathless in their shared laughter. He had to kiss her, and he did, even knowing where that would lead. After long minutes of bliss and need, when the escalating desire made her whimper and he felt the sound in his soul, he broke off the kiss. "Let me take you home."

"Yes." Her fingers tightened in his hair, tugging in a way that was all the sexier because he was sure she hadn't done it consciously. She pressed herself closer to him, soft breasts against hard chest. "No—I mean, yes, but there are too many people at my house. Where are you staying?"

Maggie's.

Impossible. He would never bring a woman to his sister's guest bedroom, anyway, but with a ten-week-old in the house, either Maggie or her husband were up every three hours. Sleep was a precious commodity there, which was why he'd booked himself a hotel by the airport in Kalispell.

Yes. He'd forgotten for a second that he'd booked that hotel after staying with his sister the night before. He'd done it to be kind, wanting to make his predawn flight without waking Maggie and her family in the morning. Kindness was paying off. He could take Kristen to the hotel. They'd have a few hours of bliss, maybe catch an hour of sleep and then…

Damn it. It wouldn't work. He'd rise and pack his things, turn his rental car in at the airport and board the plane to begin ten hours of travel. He couldn't leave Kristen in a hotel room twenty-five miles away from Rust Creek Falls. It failed every test on every level.

The fantasy disappeared in a puff of imaginary smoke. The day was over. This was not his real life, and he couldn't make love to Kristen Dalton as if it were the start of something essential. He was leaving.

"What is it?" she asked. Headlights illuminated her face for a brief second as a car drove through the intersection beyond the church and town hall. Another followed close behind, driving away from the park now that the Fourth of July was over.

He let go of her shirt—his shirt—and walked her back to the sidewalk. "My flight is early out of Kalispell. God knows I don't want to go, but I have to. I've got commitments."

"We've still got tonight."

"To make love?"

"Nothing less."

His blunt question hadn't fazed her. *Nothing less* made him want her more fiercely than ever, but what he wanted was not what was best for her.

"And then what? I'll kiss you goodbye and leave you in a hotel bed by the airport, with no way to get home, and no promise that I'll ever come back."

She winced at that picture. A pickup truck turned onto Main Street and drove past them.

"Kristen, that's not going to happen. You're not the kind of woman who wants a one-night stand, but when I don't know what I'm going to do with my future, I can't promise you anything different."

"Like you said, that's not going to happen." Her soft hand rested on his jaw, so tenderly that it didn't cause him any pain despite taking that hit from the horse earlier. "You've got the heart of a true cowboy."

If today had shown him anything, it was that he wasn't a small-town rancher at all. "A true cowboy? What does that mean?"

"A true cowboy lives by a code that isn't so different from a knight's code of chivalry. You won't make a promise you can't keep. You're telling me that you won't sleep with me tonight because you can't stay the whole night and see me safely home? That's the most caring, romantic thing I've ever heard." She gave his chest a light smack and sighed with regret. "It's sexually frustrating at the moment, but romantic."

Her talk of cowboy hearts would only keep them both in this Montana fantasy. He needed to act like the lawyer he was and cut to the facts.

"We've found something amazing today, Ryan. This isn't going to disappear in the morning."

"But I am."

She flinched. If he'd ever needed proof that lawyers could be bastards, there it was. She withdrew her hand and looked at him with a little frown of reproach. "You don't need to drive that point home. I get it."

A passing car's headlights cast her shadow on the sidewalk and stretched it to the church steps beyond. Ryan didn't trust himself to speak.

"I understand that your job isn't the kind you can just leave on a moment's notice. I know it won't be easy for you to break away for a while, but once you've fulfilled all your commitments, you'll come back. I'll be waiting for you right here in Rust Creek Falls."

Her expression was open and honest and her words were full of promise. It was all too good to be true. Or rather, it was all too good. Nothing good lasted very long. He knew it, but judging by her hopeful blue eyes, she did not.

"I haven't made a decision. You shouldn't wait for me."

She bowed her head briefly, and his heart ached for hurting her.

"I'm sorry," he began, but she cut him off.

"Please don't. I don't want you to say anything that

will make you feel bad while we're apart." She looked over her shoulder at the cars and trucks that drove through the intersection, then nodded to herself a little sadly. "Here's what I think. This magic between you and me isn't going to disappear. I will still want you next week, and next month, and the month after that. You go and take care of whatever you need to take care of, then make your list and tally up your check marks. I have faith in you, Ryan. I'm going to leave now, while our day is still perfect and I can do it without falling apart."

She rose up on her toes and kissed him, hard and quick, on the mouth. "Hurry and come back. I miss you already." She turned and started walking away.

Ryan was so dumbfounded she was out of arm's reach before he called out, "Wait!"

She spun around, hope in her expression.

It was a hope he didn't feel. "I'll drive you to your ranch."

She plastered on a smile that looked almost genuine. "There's no need. At least a dozen people who are going my way will drive past me at the corner and give me a lift. It's a small town, remember? Being able to hitch a ride is a definite check in the plus column."

Then she turned around again, and this time, he let her go.

She'd be better off without some outsider from LA interfering with her secure life and her small-town dreams. Still wearing his shirt, she headed back to the life he'd interrupted today, a life that made her happy.

His gaze settled on the swish of her hem and the backs of her legs. *Woman Walking Away*, that was what he'd title it, if he could capture it in a photograph. He could paint it from memory, if he could stand the pain.

He was no artist. There was no way that losing Kristen after one perfect day could really hurt as much as watching his mother leave him while he'd held a snow globe in his hands. No way—but damn if it didn't feel close.

At the corner by the church, an SUV stopped and Kristen climbed in. She was gone.

A second of childish memory suddenly surfaced. He hadn't dropped that snow globe. He'd thrown it on the ground deliberately with all his three-year-old might, shattering it into a thousand pieces. This new bit of knowledge about Ryan Michaels fit Ryan Roarke. If he had a snow globe now, he'd hurl it at those church steps with all his might, too.

Ryan shoved his empty hands into his pockets and turned to walk in the opposite direction, heading toward the river that would lead him back to the park.

Back to the Porsche.

Back to reality.

Chapter Five

October

"I hate this stupid column."

Kristen let go of one side of the newspaper to flick the offensive page.

"Which one?" Kayla sat behind her on the bed, patiently working a wide-toothed comb through Kristen's hair.

"Rust Creek Ramblings. It's still going on and on about 'the power of the punch' and how many couples fell in love because of that Fourth of July reception. Ouch!"

"Sorry." Kayla was silent for a moment as she tugged a little harder at what must have been a particularly stubborn knot. "Maybe there is something to that poisoned punch theory. Don't you think it's awfully coincidental that people were acting so strangely? I mean, Will Clifton got married that night but didn't even realize it until the next morning. Our own cousin got arrested for dancing in a fountain and then fell in love with the police officer. That's a pretty crazy way to fall in love. Then Levi and Claire—"

"Levi and Claire were already married." Kristen snapped the paper shut and glowered at her sister's reflection in her dresser's mirror.

"Well, they're even more in love now."

If that stupid punch had made everyone realize who their true love was, then why hadn't Ryan come back yet? He'd drunk the punch with her. Kristen tossed the newspaper facedown onto her comforter.

"I need to get the bobby pins." Kayla went into the bathroom they shared in the sprawling log house on the Circle D, the same ranch house they'd lived in all their lives. The bathroom connected their individual bedrooms. It had double sinks and enough counter space for two women to keep all the cosmetics and accessories they could need. Their brothers had dubbed their mini suite "the girls' wing" years ago, and they'd kept away even after the fiercely pink *Keep Out* signs had been outgrown.

Kristen and each of her siblings had inherited land within the Circle D. Her brother Jonah, who had the advantage of being an architect, had designed and built a log cabin on his share, but Kristen and Kayla still lived in the girls' wing of the main ranch house. Owning land was not the same thing as having the money to build a house on the land.

Someday, she'd build her own house. Maybe someday would arrive when Ryan did.

"Okay, let's do this." Kayla returned to toss a card of bobby pins onto the newspaper. She plopped herself down behind Kristen and picked up the comb again.

Kristen moved the bobby pins to read the back page. An ad for next year's rodeo season taunted her. This year's season was already over. June, July and August were the touring months in the northwest for the professional rodeo, summer months that had come and gone.

Where was Ryan?

She wasn't surprised that he hadn't come knocking on her door in July. He'd told her that he had commitments to keep. He'd said it with regret, but people were relying on him. Rodeo riders signed contracts at the beginning of the season, after all, and contracts had to be honored.

The entire month of August, she'd hoped the tour would bring him back her way, close enough to visit her between rodeos. She'd looked up schedules and wondered which towns he was choosing to compete in, but no one named Ryan Michaels appeared in any of the events within a day's drive of Rust Creek Falls. Although she ached to see him again, she hadn't been too worried. The bigger rodeos with the bigger prize money were in the cities farther away. In September, when the season was over, he would come.

Every day in September, she'd dressed with care. Every single day, because every day had been the day Ryan might return.

But now, somehow, it was October.

Without warning, tears stung her eyes, an ambush she couldn't defend against, a sign that she was losing her faith in Ryan. She hated these odd moments where the voice of doubt would suddenly seem to be the voice of reason. *Face the facts: he's not coming back.*

She sniffed the tears back. She would pummel that voice into silence.

"Am I hurting you?" Kayla asked. "I'm so sorry. I'm just trying to get all these tangles out."

"It's okay," Kristen mumbled, too cowardly to admit the truth. Of all the people on the planet, Kayla was the last one who'd chastise her for holding on to her cowboy dream, but Kayla could look at a calendar and see what everyone else saw. Kristen liked to believe that Kayla looked at her with empathy...but that look was getting darned close to pity.

If Kayla looked at her with real pity, that would mean no one, not even Kristen's twin, believed that she'd mattered to Ryan as much as he'd mattered to her.

He's coming back. Even if he was too stubborn to see how many check marks were in the plus column, he wants me. He'll try to talk me into moving to wherever he chose to settle down. He's coming back.

In the meantime, she wasn't being entirely open and honest with Kayla, for the first time in their lives. She was acting, pretending that she wasn't eaten up with worry over Ryan, going entire weeks without mentioning his name, just to avoid that final, hope-killing look of pity.

"This is going to look so good on you." Kayla held up a picture of a beautiful ice skater from a Victorian Christmas card. Kayla's mission was to make Kristen's hair look just like the Victorian ideal of feminine beauty, because Kristen was auditioning for a role in Charles Dickens's *A Christmas Carol*. The play would open Thanksgiving weekend at one of the theaters in

Kalispell, and Kristen fervently hoped it would open with her in the role of Ebenezer Scrooge's former fiancée.

The thought of returning to the stage revived her sagging spirits. There were boards to be trod, greasepaint to be smelled and shows that had to go on. The theater was her passion, and although the principal at the high school wouldn't let her direct an after-school drama club, she wasn't going to give up something she loved any longer.

In July and August and September, as she'd relived every second of her time with Ryan, one moment that had nothing to do with love had kept running through her head. *It must be frustrating to have gotten that college degree and then not use it.* She'd majored in theater because she loved the theater. She had talent. She was trained. And most of all, she missed it. The lack of a theater in Rust Creek Falls might be her own check mark in the minus column, but the fact that the city of Kalispell was within commuting distance was a plus she intended to use.

Today, she was going to pursue something that made her happy. After Kayla finished making her look like a Victorian sweetheart, Kristen was going to drive the forty-five minutes to Kalispell and kill that audition. It was time to get a job doing what she loved.

She had Ryan to thank for inspiring her. She'd thank him in person, when he came to see her. It was October, so now he would come.

"Listen to this."

Kristen set down her half-empty cup and plopped her chin in her hand, prepared to listen to her sister.

"'Sunday, November first. The Power of the Punch has claimed another love match. During the fateful Fourth of July wedding of Braden and Jennifer Traub, Brad Crawford appeared to many to be impervious to the potent properties of the now-infamous punch, but the Rambler asserts that had he not partaken, or more to the point, if his fellow poker players had not partaken of the punch, then he would not have won the piece of property that included his prospective bride.'"

"How can you read that column?" Kristen asked. "It's torture."

Kayla frowned at her over the edge of the newspaper. "It is not. You just don't like it because you're never mentioned in it. You ought to be happy about that."

Of all the things Kristen felt, happiness was not one of them. Oh, sure, she'd been pursuing it. She'd landed that role in the play. She'd even managed to move out of her childhood home.

It wasn't enough.

She pushed her coffee cup away. At least she felt some pride that it was her own coffee cup, and she was sitting at her own kitchen table in her own house. Kayla had stopped in to share her first Sunday morning brunch in Kristen's new home.

Well, it was sort of her new home. Jonah had bought a block of five Victorian homes after the flood. They'd been dirt cheap, because no one else had dared to attempt to rehab century-old houses. Jonah had turned the home on the corner lot into his architectural firm's office. The other four houses were works in progress, and Kristen was going to be part of that progress.

She was proud of her new job in the Christmas play, but the commute from the ranch to Kalispell was over an hour and a half, round trip. The ranch was north of Rust Creek Falls, but Jonah's houses were on the south edge of town, close to the highway to Kalispell. Living here saved her hours and hours of driving every week.

She couldn't pay Jonah much rent. Regional theater was run mostly on donations and volunteers. She was lucky that her role paid anything at all, but it worked out to less than minimum wage when she counted up her hours. Living here was her second job. Instead of rent, she'd agreed to scrape and sand and repaint the interior of the house for Jonah while she lived in it.

Having her own place should have been exciting, and Kristen was certain she'd been performing her role of independent young woman admirably, fooling everyone. No one except Kayla suspected the truth she was masking: she was on the edge of a horrible heartbreak, clinging as best she could to her belief that she and Ryan belonged together. Her sister's empathy had evolved into concern this month. Concern was so very close to pity.

Kayla lowered the paper to peer at her once more. "I finished the rest of the column. It's not horrible, but I think the Rambler might have used the letter *p* just a bit too much, playing off the 'power of the punch.' Was that the part that tortured you?"

Kristen shook her head.

I can't do this. I can't pretend anymore.

"What part bothered you?" Her sister was waiting, no pity in her expression…yet.

"The part that said 'Sunday, November first.'" Kristen choked out her words. "He isn't ever coming back, is he?"

Then she put her head down on the kitchen table and cried.

* * *

The phone wouldn't stop ringing.

In the inner sanctum of Ryan's office, it was only a blinking light on the phone on his desk. Screening calls was his assistant's job, so Ryan could work without interruption. But his assistant was not here, and the incessant noise from the phone in the outer office had broken Ryan's concentration. He answered the damned phone.

"Roarke speaking."

"Roarke speaking here, too."

"Hey, Dad." Ryan tossed his pen onto his desk and sat back in his chair. "What can I do for you?"

"It's November first. You know what that means."

Ryan tried to recall which sporting events were nearby. "It means you're calling me from the PGA tournament at Newport Beach."

"It means it's Sunday. A day of rest. Part of the weekend. What are you doing in the office, son?"

Ryan rubbed his jaw. It had turned slightly black and blue the day after the horse had butted him in Montana. Everyone in LA had assumed he'd been hit by a model's jealous ex. In a nod to his boxing reputation, friends and acquaintances had been equally sure the other guy must look worse. Ryan the Player, everyone's favorite hero. Never would they have guessed he'd been hit by a pure white horse attached to a white-ribboned carriage.

That day had changed him. If he'd skated close to the edge of being a Casanova before Montana, then he'd been a monk ever since. No one noticed; men still clapped him on the back in approval and women competed for his attention in vain. People saw what they wanted to see.

Except his dad.

"You haven't taken a weekend off since when? July?"

Ryan had a feeling his dad knew exactly when. "Somewhere around then. I'm not putting in a full day here. Just a few hours."

"Then meet me at the club. It'll do you good."

Golf was his dad's thing, not Ryan's. Boxing, surfing, those were Ryan's preferred leisure activities. Actually, he hadn't been surfing since July, either. The boxing, though, he'd used like a drug for the past four months, throwing punches until his brain was numb, almost wishing for a hard hit to knock all the thoughts out of his head.

"Humor me. Come hit a bucket of balls with your old man."

Ryan supposed the fresh air would do him good. When he showed up at the club's driving range, he got much more than that.

"Your mother and I have been having some serious discussions about the future of the firm."

Thwack. Damn if his father couldn't make those balls sail. Ryan chose an iron from his golf bag and addressed the ball that had been teed up for him by a trendy automated machine.

"We want to retire earlier than our original timeline."

Ryan ignored the ball and turned to address his father instead. "Have you had some news I should be aware of?"

A week after Ryan's trip to Montana, his father had driven himself to the hospital with chest pain. He'd escaped any permanent damage beyond being chastised by his wife and son for not calling an ambulance, but the doctors had labeled it a wake-up call. It had been one for Ryan, as well. There was no way he could abandon his parents and their law firm for a Montana dream. The whole idea of living in a cowboy town had been a whim, anyway.

Kristen had been real.

Real, and out of his reach.

"I'm as healthy as a horse," his dad said. "But that's the point. I'd like to take my wife around the world while we're healthy enough and young enough to enjoy it. That's always been one of our goals."

Ryan felt the weight of the firm settle on his shoulders as he turned back to the tee. His parents deserved the good life, and to give it to them, Ryan would become the only Roarke in Roarke and Associates. They'd groomed him to take over someday, and he was ready. It didn't matter if that day came now or ten years from now.

I will still want you next month, and the month after that.

Kristen's words were never far from his mind. If Ryan followed in his father's footsteps and retired a few years early, he could move to Montana, guilt-free, in thirty years. That would be swell, if Kristen still wanted him thirty years from now.

Thwack. Ryan sent the ball on a long, hard drive.

His father approved. "Nice hit. We should think about beefing up the Associates part of Roarke and Associates before we retire. We're not trying to burden you any more than you already burden yourself. What do you think about offering partnership to Lori?"

The next ball had been teed up for him. Ryan knocked the holy hell out of it with his nine-iron. "We'd be smart to make Lori a partner whether you retire or not. We'll still need to hire an additional attorney. I'll start the headhunt."

"When? You're already working seven days a week."

Ryan readied himself for another swing, but his father reached across the low wall that partitioned the driving range and placed his hand on Ryan's shoulder.

"Let me tell you another one of my life's goals. I want my children to outlive me. That might make me a selfish old bastard, but I think I deserve to leave this earth without seeing you or Shane or Maggie leave it first. Every parent deserves that, whether they get it or not."

"What the—for God's sake, Dad. What kind of talk is this?"

"You're scaring me, Ryan. No one works as many hours as you've been doing and lives to tell the tale. Whatever demon you're trying to exorcise with work is winning. You need to try something else. Find a healthier way to forget whatever it is you're trying to forget."

Forgetting Montana and its breathtaking scenery, he could do. Forgetting the ideal of living in a small town, forgetting what it was like to belong to a community, all of that he could do. They'd been pipe dreams, Norman Rockwell pictures that were too perfect to be real.

Forgetting Kristen? He couldn't.

He'd been trying to adopt a brotherly attitude toward her. He was watching out for her best interests by staying away. She had a better chance at finding happiness in life and love with a cowboy who'd grown up where she had. She needed a man who understood ranches and horses and that pace of life. It was better for her if he stayed away. He'd learn to deal with it.

"I mean it, Ryan. You're working yourself into an early grave."

Ryan traded his nine-iron for his driver, a better club for beating the crap out of an inanimate object. "This is serious talk."

"It is. Now lighten up." His dad clapped him on the shoulder one last time and stepped back to his own tee. "Go home. Vegetate. Take a pretty girl out to dinner." Under his breath, he added, "Today."

Ryan looked in the direction his father was looking. He recognized the actress, and she recognized him. She changed direction immediately, walking toward him in her white golf skirt like she was walking down a fashion show runway. She had the legs and the attitude to pull it off.

"Ryan Roarke. It's been too long." Her hug enveloped him in perfume. Her civilized cheek kiss landed just a little too close to his ear, suggesting more of a lover's nibble on an earlobe than a meeting of friends. He got the message.

She'd sent him that message before. When word had leaked out that he may have done some work for a Tarantino or a DeNiro, rumors that he would never confirm or deny as part of his professional code, the constant stream of hopeful actresses had become a deluge. That was Hollywood. He wondered what rumor she'd heard this time.

Thwack.

"I've got a secret," she cooed. "I'm doing a screen test tomorrow. Isn't that exciting? It's all hush-hush, but you probably already know it's something for Century Films."

He said nothing. It wasn't necessary.

She placed her finger on her full, lower lip, pretending to be lost in thought. "Come to think of it, you introduced me to the man they've tapped to be the assistant director. He was in our little group when we took that trip to Carmel. Wasn't that a fun weekend?"

Thwack.

"You know, if you wanted to go back, I'm free this coming weekend. Who else was there last time? We could call around and get everyone together again."

"Especially the assistant director."

She perched on the bench that held his gear, crossing one long leg over the other and swinging her foot. "That would be such a boost for me. If you could arrange it, I wouldn't know how to thank you." The low purr of her voice and the come-be-naughty-with-me curve of her smile meant she knew exactly how she'd thank him.

Ryan looked at her, and wished for someone else. "I'm not available this weekend."

She didn't give up easily, but after some pointless banter, she did give up. Ryan had no doubt she'd find some other way to refresh her contacts with the assistant director and anyone else who could give her an inside edge to win the role.

"Not this time, then?"

Not ever.

She left him with another perfumed kiss, too smart to burn any bridges. As she sauntered away, Ryan's father continued working on his golf swing, as if he hadn't paid attention at all to what was happening on his son's side of the partition.

Ryan answered his unspoken question, anyway. "Not my idea of relaxation."

His father only grunted in a neutral way that could have meant anything.

Ryan began working his way through another dozen golf balls in silence. He wasn't interested in relationships that served careers any more than he was interested in the ones that were merely convenient. For the past four months of his life, he hadn't been interested in anything. Not in the golf or surfing that were the hallmarks of Southern California. Not in the endless summer of Los Angeles, and worst of all, not in running Roarke and Associates.

The pursuit of happiness, Ryan Roarke's personal pursuit of happiness, had led him to Montana. He'd fallen in love under the blue sky while looking into Kristen Dalton's blue eyes.

Fallen in love.

Thwack.

He'd fallen in love, and then he'd gone away and stayed away. Although Kristen had smiled and said she wasn't worried, he'd hurt her in those last few moments. If his father thought his son was leading a punishing life, Ryan saw some justice in it. He'd been treating himself badly because he'd treated someone else badly.

He didn't know if Kristen was hurting still. Perhaps she'd moved on.

Perhaps she hadn't.

He had no way to find out, short of making an ass of himself on the phone with his sister. Maggie worked in Rust Creek Falls's one law office for an attorney named Dalton. In a town that size, Dalton had to be related to Kristen somehow. If Kristen had been sad or depressed and told her family it was because Ryan had broken her heart, then Maggie would have heard about it. Kristen obviously hadn't been talking about him.

Brad Crawford, an acquaintance from the flood recovery days, had consulted him about land deeds last month. Ryan had resisted the temptation to ask about Kristen. Brad would have wondered why the heck Ryan Roarke was asking about one of the Dalton girls. Clearly, Rust Creek Falls wasn't buzzing with rumors that Kristen was brokenhearted over the man she'd spent the Fourth of July with, and Ryan would do nothing to stir up gossip where none currently existed.

No news was good news. It meant Kristen was fine without him.

Thwack. As fast as the automated range teed up the balls, he hit them, full force, full swing, full power. *Thwack. Thwack.*

"What's wrong, son?" His father was resting both arms on the wall, all pretense that he was doing anything but worry about his son completely dropped.

I miss her.

"Nothing, Dad."

Ryan needed to see Kristen again, if only to verify for himself that she was doing fine without him. He wanted what was best for her, so he'd have no peace until he was sure she was happy.

"I want to go back. To Montana."

His dad raised one brow, a move Ryan realized he'd adopted himself, long ago. "Your sister and Shane are bringing their families here for Thanksgiving in just a couple of weeks."

"I know. I need to see—I need the change of scene. I'll tie everything up this week and fly out Saturday.

One more document for Crawford came across my desk this week. I'll handle it while I'm there."

His father didn't ask any questions or point out that an overnight courier would be more efficient than an attorney flying to another state.

"Have a good trip, son. Get done what you need to do."

Chapter Six

Date night.

Maggie Roarke Crawford had been looking forward to this all week. She'd even loaded her sweet little Madeline into the car this morning, driven all the way to Kalispell and gotten her hair done for the event. Seven months after having her baby, some of her most chic outfits fit again. Tonight, she felt a little blonder, a little sexier and more than a little ready to paint the town red. She and her husband, Jesse, had hired a babysitter and headed out to the hottest spot in town: the high school gym.

On Friday nights, when it wasn't basketball season, of course, the gym became the town movie theater. Maggie loved it. It was a little like watching a movie in one's living room with extended family, since a sizable portion of the town always showed up. Gossip abounded at the refreshment stand. At the end of the night, the moviegoers all helped stack the chairs.

Tonight's double feature had started with a romance that was replete with tear-worthy moments. Maggie was pretty sure her husband had started out hating it, but midway through, when the emotional scenes on the screen had made her sigh and cling to his hand with both of hers, he'd relaxed and settled in for the duration.

The second show was going to be the opposite, an action-adventure film full of explosions and cars. Maggie felt the need to stock up on chocolate in preparation. Apparently, so did most of the women of Rust Creek Falls, because the line for the concession stand was an almost exclusively female gathering. Everyone was talking about the romantic movie and its handsome leading man.

Her youngest sister-in-law, Natalie Crawford, was behind her in line, gushing about the movie's ending to Ben Dalton's twin nieces. Maggie turned around to join in the conversation.

"Omigosh, wasn't that the most romantic proposal at the end?" Natalie asked. "I think I'd be willing to go through the wringer just to have a proposal like that. Everything turned out all right."

"That proposal happened in the nick of time," said one of the twins. "If he'd done one more jerky thing, I don't think any kind of proposal could have convinced me to marry him."

Maggie wasn't sure which twin was Kristen and which was Kayla—they looked so much alike—but she agreed with the sentiment. "It was lucky for him that all his jerky things were done to save an orphanage. We can forgive a guy who's trying to save children."

"Plus, he had washboard abs," Natalie added with a wink.

"Yes, there's that," Maggie laughed. "Jerks should strive to at least have washboard abs."

Kristen-Kayla, the one who'd been talking, suddenly pressed the back of her hand to her mouth and made a distressed sound. For a second, Maggie thought she'd sneezed or choked, but no, that had been a sob.

"Ohmigosh, Kristen, are you okay?" Natalie asked.

The quiet twin put her arm around her sister's shoulders. "That movie was pretty sad. It had me in tears, too."

Maggie and Natalie and the one who must be Kayla instinctively clustered closer to Kristen, shielding her from public scrutiny.

"Let's scoot out of the way," Maggie suggested. "Here's a napkin."

Although Maggie didn't really know Kristen, there was an unwritten girl code that rallied them all to help. Maggie was just about to suggest they head for the ladies' room when the young woman shook her hair back and straightened her shoulders.

"I'll be fine. Really. I was just thinking that in real life, there's never an orphanage to explain things away, is there?"

Oh, dear. The poor thing had obviously had her heart broken. Maggie sympathized. "I'm afraid when real guys do jerky things, it usually just means they're jerks."

"Is this about the airline pilot?" Natalie asked Kayla, who gave a quick negative shake of her head.

But Kristen did one of those half laugh, half sobs. "It might as well be. I'm starting to think they're all the same. I was dumb enough to believe the pilot when he said he hated to leave. Now I know he was having a grand time seeing his other girlfriends. You'd think I would have wised up, but no. A handsome cowboy comes through town and I actually believe him when he says he hates to leave me, but he must. They always must go, simply must. I even believed that he was going to come back when the rodeo tour was over."

"A rodeo star?" Natalie was clearly dying for more details.

Maggie felt badly for Kristen, who was slowly shredding her napkin.

"I thought a cowboy would be different. He'd love his family more than anything else, and be loyal to his lady. He seemed to be a real gentleman, too."

Natalie frowned. "Yeah, but a rodeo star is a different kind of cowboy."

"He made it sound like this was his final season, because he was looking to settle down here in Rust Creek Falls. I'm such a sucker."

Kayla gave her twin a squeeze. "I would have fallen for the man, too. The stories he told you were so poignant, who wouldn't have?"

Maggie smiled to herself at the sister's show of loyalty. Shane and Ryan had always been loyal to her like that, too.

"He fed you more lies?" Natalie shook her head. "Men are pigs."

Maggie tried to temper that kind of blanket statement. It went against her mind-set as an attorney to accept a stereotype as a legitimate argument. "Let's just say if a man acts like a pig, there's almost never a justification. Kristen had it right. They're never protecting a secret orphanage in real life."

"Thanks, guys." Kristen kept tearing the napkin into pieces and crumpling the strips in her palm. "The thing is, I still don't think he lied. If he'd bragged that he owned a fancy sports car, that would be one thing, but what would be the point in telling me he was adopted? He remembered his first mother. She left him when he was three. Just walked away and left him."

That got Maggie's attention. One of her adopted brothers had been abandoned when he was three. What a strange coincidence for this rodeo rider to have been left like that, too.

"I'm sure he made it up to get pity points. What a scum bucket." Natalie gave Kristen a friendly bump, hip to hip. "Did he at least have washboard abs?"

Kristen laughed a little as she dabbed her nose with the crumbled napkin. "He did. I mean, I didn't take his shirt off, but he was rock hard when I hugged him."

This elicited some snickering from Natalie.

"He was a good dancer. Tall. Handsome. Nice voice, nice manners." The hint of a smile lit Kristen's face as she remembered the better traits of her rodeo star. The poor girl was still carrying a torch for this guy. Maggie was glad she had lots of support from a loving sister and from Natalie, too.

Maggie started looking around the gym for her husband, getting ready to graciously bow out of this circle now that the tears were under control. Natalie was settling in for the juicy details, and although Maggie was only a few years older than they were, she was starting to feel like the odd man out as an old married woman. These three were all single and had gone to school together.

Maggie craned her neck a bit, trying to spot her husband. Married women had benefits, and hers was Jesse Crawford.

"Where did you meet him?" Natalie asked. "Is he famous? Would I recognize his name?"

"I don't think so. It's Ryan Michaels. I met him here in town on the Fourth of July."

"The 'power of the punch,' eh?"

Maggie snapped her attention back to Kristen. Her brother was Roarke, not Michaels, but he'd been here for the Fourth of July. A man named Ryan, in town for the Fourth of July, who'd been abandoned at age three? It couldn't be.

"I don't know about the punch. I wish I had an excuse for being so gullible a second time." Kristen's hands doubled into fists. "I believed everything he said. He just about broke my heart with his story. He painted this whole picture about how she left him standing on the steps to a church—just *terrible*. It's over the top, right? I should have seen that, right? At the time, I felt so special that he was telling me something so personal, but it was just a line to make women want to comfort him. It worked."

Dear God, church steps. She was talking about Ryan. Her brother Ryan had broken this sweet girl's heart.

Frantically, Maggie thought back to the Fourth of July. They'd all gone to the wedding together, but Madeline had only been about ten weeks old, and she and Jesse had taken the baby home to nap. They'd all fallen asleep. Later, it had seemed like too much trouble to cart the stroller and diaper bag and the rest back to the park. She'd assumed Ryan had renewed an acquaintance from the flood recovery days, but he must have struck up a flirtation with Kristen. It all made sense, except why on earth had he told this poor girl he was in the rodeo? It was flabbergasting.

Maggie felt physically sick. Ryan had always been a lady-killer, but this wasn't LA, and Kristen wasn't a starlet. How could he? But he had, he clearly had, and now Kristen's spurt of anger was over and tears were welling up in her eyes again.

"The thing is, and please don't think I'm crazy or a complete idiot for thinking this, but the thing is, what if his story was real? He probably has a hard time trusting anyone. Maybe he does want to be with me, but his childhood affected him so that he doesn't believe a woman would love him. Or…oh, I don't know. What if he was injured, and he's been in a hospital this whole time? What do you think?"

I think I'm going to kill my brother.

But first, she needed to give Kristen some immediate advice. "Here's what I think you should do. You should get back in line and buy yourself a serious amount of chocolate, and you should avoid sad movies for a while. The next movie will be all car explosions and no plot. It's perfect." Impulsively, Maggie gave Kristen a hug and whispered in her ear. "Try not to drive yourself crazy with questions that have no answer."

Maggie left to find her husband. She had the rest of date night to salvage. First thing tomorrow morning, she would give Ryan a piece of her mind. Poor Kristen might not be able to get any answers, but Maggie would.

"Get your butt up here. Now. This minute."

"Good morning to you, too, Maggie. Nice of you to call."

Ryan clamped his phone between his shoulder and ear and hoisted his suitcase into the overhead bin. The noise of a couple of hundred people boarding the airplane gave him a certain amount of privacy to talk with Maggie before takeoff. She'd probably hear the background noise and guess where he was, but in the meantime, he could have some fun with her.

"Why would I come see you? Isn't it snowing there? Not to rub it in, but I was golfing with Dad this week. Scratch that. I am definitely rubbing it in."

Ryan took his first-class seat and waved away the flight attendant's offer of a drink. Strangers with backpacks and luggage and kids continued to file past.

"I'm not joking around, Ryan. You have to come up here."

Her tone of voice alarmed him. Ryan tuned out everything but his sister. "What's wrong? Are you at the hospital? Jesse or Madeline sick?"

"You're the sick one. You broke a girl's heart last time you were in Rust Creek Falls, you jerk."

He nearly dropped the phone.

"I was at the movies last night, talking to Kristen Dalton at the concession stand."

The name exploded in his brain. He hadn't heard anyone say her name, not once in all these months. She'd been only his own silent wish, his own secret memory. Hearing his sister speak about her was jarring, a sudden reminder that Kristen wasn't his private fantasy. She was a real woman with friends and family. A woman who lived a normal life and went to movies.

"She was in tears. The movie was sad, and it made her cry, and do you know why? Because you're extra sensitive when your heart's been broken. Kristen Dalton! Oh, Ryan, how could you?"

Kristen crying, brokenhearted—Ryan's own heart stopped beating for a moment. He tightened his grip on the phone.

"She asked you about me?"

"No, she didn't ask me about you. What kind of vain question is that?"

It hadn't been vain. It had been hopeful. He was on this plane because he'd needed to see for himself that Kristen was okay. That she'd moved on. That she was fine without him. *Closure.* He was having too hard of a time in California without it.

But now...

Ryan covered one ear and turned away from the aisle to better hear his sister. This flight connected to Kalispell through Las Vegas, and the passengers who boarded were boisterous, ready for vacation. Ryan concentrated to hear everything his sister said. Every word was crucial.

"If she didn't ask you about me, then how do you know I'm the reason she's heartbroken?" It was far more likely that she'd been dating someone else this fall. Just because Ryan couldn't stand the idea didn't mean it wasn't probable.

"Because I'm standing in line for some Twizzlers and Sno-Caps, and this really pretty woman starts pouring her heart out about a man who was adopted at age three. He's left her behind without a backward glance, that much is obvious to anyone who's listening, but she can't see that, because she's crazy about him. She's clinging to this idea that he's just afraid to believe in love after the way his mother abandoned him on church steps. And this paragon of a man that she's still hoping will come back is named Ryan."

A man that she's still hoping will come back.

The entire purpose of the flight changed in an instant. There was nothing of brotherly concern in his attitude toward Kristen. Screw closure. He wanted Kristen as he'd wanted her from the first: in his arms for a dance and a kiss. By his side for a laugh during a meal. He wanted her in his bed, and yes, he wanted to trust her with his heart.

If she wanted his heart. It had seemed unlikely after all these months, but suddenly, with his sister's words, everything he wanted and needed was possible. Everything could be his, if Kristen still wanted him. They could work out all the rest, somehow.

"You can't leave a girl hanging with her heart on her sleeve like that. She's really crazy about you, you moron. If you think you'll find a better woman down there in LA, you're wrong, but you at least owe it to Kristen to end things cleanly so she can move on."

"I don't want to end things."

"Well, you have to. It's just cruel, letting her carry a torch for you."

Hope was a painful emotion, forcing its way into a heart that hadn't allowed any room for it.

Maggie misinterpreted his silence. Of course, she only saw him as her brother, the player. It wouldn't occur to her that he'd been serious about Kristen. "I mean it, Ryan. If you don't get up here, I'll—I'll—I'll tell Mom."

Her threat cut the tension, and amazingly, Ryan found he could laugh despite the painful hope in his chest. "Don't do anything so drastic. I'm already on my way."

"Good. When you book your flight, let me know, and I'll pick you up at the airport."

"I said I'm already on my way. Listen." He held the phone away from his ear as the flight attendant repeated the announcement, which everyone ignored, about stepping out of the aisle to let others pass during boarding.

"Wait a minute. You'd already decided to come up here? Did Jesse call you last night?"

"I'd already decided last week to see Kristen. I told you I didn't want to end things, but you were too busy chewing me out to hear that."

"Wow. That's… I should get the guest room ready." She sounded a little faint.

"I'm staying at Maverick Manor. Between you, Jesse and the baby, that's three chaperones I don't need while I'm trying to woo a woman."

"Woo her? Not break up with her? Ryan, you can't do this. You can't keep letting her think you're some kind of rodeo star. The fake name, the whole cowboy masquerade—I just can't be a party to that. I'm not going to pretend I don't know you."

The flight attendant stopped directly by his seat and spoke loudly. "Excuse me, sir, but you're going to have to turn off your phone now."

"What are you talking about, Maggie?"

"Sir, I must insist. The doors have been closed."

"Sounds like you have to go," Maggie said. "I'll talk to you when you get here."

"What masquerade, damn it?"

"Sir."

"Kristen Dalton isn't in love with you. She's in love with a cowboy named Ryan Michaels. Hang up before you get kicked off that plane."

Chapter Seven

After ten agonizing hours of travel, Ryan hung up once more after talking to his sister. Numb, he sank onto the foot of the oversize bed in his room at Maverick Manor.

He hadn't done it on purpose. He'd worn cowboy boots and two-stepped to a country-western band, but he'd never said he was a cowboy. He hadn't specifically said he was an attorney from LA, either, but he'd never once talked about rodeos.

When he'd been standing by those church steps with Kristen, he'd accidentally let slip the name that he'd gone by as a preschooler. She'd apparently assumed he was still Michaels. That meant Kristen didn't know he was related to the Maggie Roarke Crawford who worked with her own uncle. She didn't know he was related to celebrity chef Shane Roarke. And she most certainly didn't know he, Ryan, defended contracts for movie studios and recording artists.

He'd wanted it that way. When they'd first met, he'd only said he was Ryan, not Ryan Roarke. He'd wanted to feel what it would be like to be a local.

The locals around here are all cowboys.

Maybe he should have foreseen that, but the locals weren't rodeo stars, damn it. He'd never been to a rodeo in his life. She'd been born and raised on a ranch. How had he fooled her so completely?

Ryan fell back onto the quilt-topped mattress.

He'd just have to level with her immediately. Like ripping off a bandage, he'd have to confess his missteps and mistakes. When he told Kristen that her humble cowboy who'd been considering a move to Rust Creek Falls was actually a high-powered Hollywood attorney who specialized in the entertainment industry, would she still want him?

He stared at the ceiling until the knots of the pine slats blurred into nothing. In their place, he saw the hem of a woman's dress, swishing with every step as she walked away.

The need to rip off a bandage was not a great motivator.

Although Ryan had spent a week rearranging his whole schedule specifically to see Kristen, he found himself stalling now that he was in Rust Creek Falls. He was dying to look into those blue eyes again, to feel her soft palm against his jaw, to run his hand down her soft hair. But first, he had to tell her that everything she thought she knew about him was wrong. She was going to be devastated. His first sight of her could be his last.

And so, after a restless night at the hotel, he spent Sunday morning doing everything except what he'd come to town to do. Instead of asking for directions to the Dalton family ranch, he located Brad Crawford and got his signature on that final piece of paperwork. Instead of knocking on Kristen's door, he stopped by Maggie's house to see the baby, who'd grown so much in four months it was astonishing.

He couldn't avoid the inevitable, but he told himself it was smart to delay it. This mistaken identity had caught him completely by surprise just twenty-four hours ago. He knew how to win a debate and he knew how to persuade a jury. Both of those things required careful preparation, and Ryan was not prepared to rip off any bandages without a plan. He needed time to think, and he needed to avoid Kristen until he was ready.

The hotel was too small for his restless pacing. He considered walking the perimeter of the park while he thought of the right words to say, but Maggie and her family were headed there. She'd become a true Montanan who thought forty degrees was perfectly balmy weather for a Sunday stroll. The park wouldn't provide any solitude.

He could retrace Kristen's tour. Walk along the river in broad daylight. Head up Main Street to that church where he'd said too much—or where he'd said too little. But revisiting the sights seemed too maudlin, too much like a scene from a sappy movie—and too risky. He might run into Kristen unprepared.

He got into the truck he'd rented and drove out of town. The highway led straight to Kalispell, right through the heart of town. Main Street was flanked by the same type of sturdy brick buildings that lined the streets of Rust Creek Falls. There, away from the Crawfords and Daltons, he parked his truck, got out and started walking.

* * *

"Let's try it again from the top of the scene. Old Scrooge and the Ghost of Christmas Past, I want you two to stand a little closer upstage." The assistant director looked over his shoulder toward the back of the theater. "Can we keep the spotlight on Old Scrooge if he moves upstage? Yes? Good."

Kristen stood motionless at center stage. This rehearsal was primarily meant to refine the blocking, deciding where every actor would move during the scene. The lighting director, the stage crew and the prop master needed to know where the actors delivered every line. It was tedious work, but part of being an actress was being patient.

Kristen hated blocking days. She got through them by using them as an acting exercise, in which she had to play the role of Patient Actress. Since Patient Actress would not tap her booted foot impatiently, Kristen stopped. She stuffed her hands in the back pockets of her jeans. They didn't wear costumes for most rehearsals, but Kristen wore a bright blue sweater with her jeans and boots, because her costume was a striking blue gown. She had her hair up in a messy bun to simulate the Victorian style she'd wear during performances. Her hair affected what angle she held her head, even which shadows the different stage lights cast on her face, so it was necessary.

"Belle, switch places with Young Ebenezer. I want Old Scrooge to be looking over his shoulder at you. He'll be seeing your face while you break his heart all over again."

Obediently, Kristen switched places with the actor who was playing Ebenezer in the prime of his life. The assistant director had one key point wrong, however.

"I'm not breaking Ebenezer's heart. He's already decided he loves money more than me. I'm the one who is brokenhearted."

She cut herself short. *I'm the one who is brokenhearted.* Saying those words out loud felt like a personal confession, although no one could know they were true for Kristen as well as Belle, the unwanted fiancée.

The assistant director flipped through the script in his hand, but he didn't stop on any page long enough to read a full line of dialogue. "We're not talking about motivation today. We're talking about lighting."

"Yes, but you want the audience to see Old Scrooge's face," Kristen persisted. "If his shoulder is to that half of the audience, they'll miss his expression. This is the moment where he realizes that letting Belle go was a mistake that ruined the rest of his life."

Again, she fell silent. She knew she was a fool for worrying about Ryan, but she wondered if he was happy now, after choosing a path that didn't include her. Last Friday, she'd said as much during movie night, but it had only earned her those terrible looks of pity from Natalie, Kayla and her uncle's partner, Maggie Crawford.

The actor playing Old Scrooge backed her up. "She's right. I'm the one who has to be devastated, not the younger me. Maybe if we stood this way—" he put his hand on Young Ebenezer's shoulders and the two of them shuffled clockwise for a few steps "—more of the house would be able to see both of our faces. There's a big contrast between what he felt then and how he feels now."

After more discussion, the assistant director left the stage to stand in the audience. He flipped through his script once more. "Okay, let's take it from, uh, Young

Ebenezer's line. 'Have I asked to be released from this promise?'"

Kristen took both of the actor's hands in hers, breathed in deeply to focus herself and then looked up at him with all the sadness of a woman who realizes her love is not returned. To become Belle, Kristen only had to admit to herself that she was unwanted. Ryan was never coming back.

Ebenezer looked at her coldly. "Have I asked to be released from this promise?"

"Not in words, no."

"How, then?"

"In the way you spend all hours in your counting house. In the way your smiles are only bestowed on the scales, when the balance of gold tilts them in your favor. Tell me truly, if you saw me today for the first time, would you make the effort to dance with me at Fezziwig's party? Would you ask your friends for an introduction to a girl who has no dowry?"

He lifted his chin sharply, his nostrils flaring in distaste at her question.

"You see?" She let the tears that welled in her eyes spill down her cheeks. "The man who loved me is only a memory. For his sake, I pray you will be happy upon your chosen path. You no longer want me to walk with you, no matter how much I wish it otherwise. Ebenezer Scrooge, I release you."

She bowed her head, and let go of Ebenezer's stiff hands.

"Okay, that's plenty." The assistant director made his way back to the stage. "That was great, by the way. Just do it twice every weekend from opening night through Christmas, okay?"

Kristen smiled obligingly, back in her role as Patient Actress, and used the cuff of her sweater to dry her cheeks.

"You make my job hard," Ebenezer said. "I'm supposed to look at you like you're as appealing as an empty wallet, but man, I just wanted to go down on my knees and beg you to stay."

"You made my job easy." Old Scrooge patted her on the shoulder with one hand and gave Ebenezer a good-natured shove with the other. "It'll be easy to call this guy out for being a fool. He really is a cold-hearted bastard if he can look in those teary blue eyes and not feel a thing. I was ready to deliver my line with gusto, if that pompous kid hadn't cut us off. When's the real director back again? Tuesday?"

"Thank you, Act Two," the assistant director called out in dismissal. "Act Three beginners, please. Act Three beginners, take your places."

Kristen made her escape into the wing. She couldn't decide if this was the worst role or best role she'd ever taken. The similarity of her situation to Belle's made for difficult rehearsals. The lines she had to speak came too close to her real feelings. She had to relive her dashed hopes over and over.

On the other hand, this role was a piece of cake for her as an actress. She had only to think of Ryan, and very little acting skill was required to give an authentic performance.

The bad news is, I got jilted. The good news is, I got great reviews.

She tried to laugh at her own joke, but the hitch in her breath was more like a sob. She felt a big, ugly cry coming on, nothing like Belle's gentle tears.

"I'm going out for some fresh air," she said to the stage manager. She threw her polka-dotted scarf around her neck and grabbed her red jacket from the folding chair where she'd thrown it three hours ago.

The stage manager checked the large clock over her station in the wings. "You might as well leave for the day. I can tell you right now we'll never make it to the final scene."

Kristen swallowed hard and faked a smile. "Thanks, Sue. See you Tuesday."

She all but ran for the stage door, barely making it outside before Patient Actress and Belle the Fiancée and every other role she'd been playing for the past four months gave way under the crushing weight of being Kristen Dalton, the girl who still wanted Ryan Michaels to come back for her.

The stores and shops of Kalispell were decked out for Christmas. Not one window or door seemed to have escaped the bonds of garland and ribbon. Despite this, Ryan could admire the brick buildings, sturdy brick squares that had withstood a century of Christmas seasons and could probably withstand a century more. He'd survive this Christmas, too. He always did, no matter what bad memories were associated with the holiday.

Ryan tucked his hands deeply in the pockets of his wool overcoat. It was double-breasted and sharply tailored, because he was not a cowboy and not pretending to be one. It was full-length, because he was from Los Angeles and the weather here was flirting with freezing, but it was also open in front because he'd been walking for block after block, building up heat. If the coat flared behind him like a cowboy's duster, he couldn't help it. Let people think what they wanted.

Except Kristen. What she *wanted* to think about him mattered. She wanted a cowboy. He kept running the scenarios in his mind, but no matter how he presented the basic facts, he couldn't imagine her face lighting up in one of her dazzling smiles. *Oh, you're actually living in a megalopolis over one thousand miles away? Fantastic!*

The cold November wind had cleared his mind and cooled his expectations. The truth was, she'd fallen in love with a rodeo rider because that was who she'd wanted to fall in love with. That was not him. He thought she was perfect as she was, a simple ranch girl, born and bred in a small town, but nothing good lasted for long. There was no real chance that he and Kristen could still be a couple after he told her the truth. Her feelings for him would be crushed in an instant, and all the glitter and magic would drain away.

Like a damned shattered snow globe.

He stopped walking, and stood on the cold sidewalk, letting the north wind blow away the childish vision— all gone, bye-bye. He turned on his heel to head back to his SUV. It was time to go face Kristen.

Kristen.

She stood on the sidewalk before him, perhaps twenty yards away, staring into a store window, a beautiful mirage for a man who hadn't realized just how much of a desert his life had become. He drank up the sight of her. How had he survived the deprivation?

She seemed tired, her shoulders low and her expression downcast. When the brisk wind pulled more tendrils loose from her pinned-up hair, she didn't seem to have the energy to turn her collar up.

He knew, somehow, he'd looked just as tired moments ago, before seeing her. He'd denied them both the chance to be happy. She had the right to be furious with him for causing her pain.

"Kristen." Her name was little more than a whisper, the apology he owed her too big for words.

She tucked a wisp of hair behind her ear and turned away, light and graceful in all her moves despite the sadness in her expression. When she turned her back on him and he lost sight of her face, something in him snapped. She had to go; he understood that. Nothing good lasted forever. But he couldn't let her walk away without telling her how grateful he was for the most perfect summer day of his life.

"Kristen!"

She looked over her shoulder. Their gazes met, and her blue eyes opened wide the moment she recognized him.

He took one step toward her, another, and then he realized she was smiling—smiling at *him*—and he was running. She came flying toward him, and he opened his arms wide and swooped her off her feet. Momentum carried them around and around as she laughed.

"You came back, you came back," she said, her arms tight around his neck.

He had her lifted high, so his face was buried in her playful scarf and loose hair for a long, blinding moment of reunion that needed no words. Then she slid down his body, until her cowboy boots touched the ground.

She kept his face in both her hands, smoothing her thumbs across his cheekbones. She was beaming at him, every bit as stunning as he'd remembered, yet ten times more vivid in person than a memory could ever be.

"You look amazing. Even more beautiful than I remembered, and I think of you every day as the most beautiful woman I know." He was babbling. He didn't care.

"I can't believe you're real," she said, exactly what he was feeling. "We never took a photo that day. Neither one of us brought a phone. You can't imagine how much I've wished I just had a picture of you—"

The catch in her voice made him catch her close again, holding her against his chest within the open folds of his coat. "I'm sorry. I'm so very sorry. I shouldn't have stayed away so long."

She nuzzled into the side of his throat. "You must have had a good reason."

Her faith in him was humbling. And misplaced.

You have to tell her the truth.

"I've been working." He rested his cheek on top of her head, regret in every syllable. "In California."

"California?" She picked her head up. Stepped back.

Ryan braced himself. The bandage ripping had begun. He'd known since Maggie's bombshell that it would come down to this. He'd never hated having to do something more.

"No wonder I couldn't find you." She bit her lip and looked up at him apologetically. "I kept checking the Montana papers for event results. Then it occurred to me to look at Wyoming. I might have gotten desperate enough to check out Idaho's results on the web a few times. Pretty bad, huh? But it never occurred to me to look at California."

He had to look away from those trusting blue eyes. "I didn't deserve to have you looking so hard for me."

"Did you come from California all the way back to Montana just to see me?"

"Yes, I did." She deserved to know the truth in this, as well. He wanted her to know he'd suffered, too, although it had been his own fault. "I was going crazy, wondering how you were. I missed you."

Kristen made a quick movement of her hands toward his face, and for a split second, he thought a slap was coming. He deserved a slap. Instead, with two hands in his hair, she pulled him to her, and kissed him. Hard. Hungry.

No memory could wake every cell in his body like this. He was alive, all sensation. The feel of Kristen in his arms, the smell of her skin, the very taste of her, each were their own small miracle. It didn't matter if he deserved her kiss; he was greedy for it and took what she gave him, savoring the connection that made him want to be closer still.

A passing truck honked a horn, whether in criticism or approval didn't matter. It was enough to bring Ryan back to the real world. He lifted his head to study Kristen's face and felt utterly satisfied with how thoroughly kissed her mouth looked and how perfectly pink her cheeks were. She rocked back on her heels—she'd been standing on tiptoe during the entire kiss—and gripped his arms for a moment as she regained her equilibrium.

She looked so feminine, so delicate, but then she smiled like a woman who knew a secret. "Someday, we are going to kiss when we are alone and indoors, somewhere very private, and things are going to burn so far out of control you won't be safe from me any longer."

He could've dropped to his knees on the sidewalk. She was so Kristen, so boldly herself. He wanted her.

Hell, he had her. She wasn't playing coy or shy or mysterious. She was thrilled to see him, as eager to pick up where they'd left off as he was.

But the hell of it was, he couldn't keep her. He wasn't the man she thought he was.

Rip off the bandage.

Not here. Not on a sidewalk in the center of town.

He tried to use humor to ease the sexual tension she'd just ratcheted into high gear. "There's a traditional order to these things. I think you're supposed to buy me a drink first. I passed a bakery not too far back. Maybe they sell coffee."

Her smile only deepened. "They do, but if you're daring enough to cut through the alley with me, there's a diner that serves amazing pie one street over. You'd be indoors with me for the first time, but I think you'll be safe if I have a nice slice of homemade pie competing for my attention."

She led the way through the alley. From behind, she made a colorful picture. Her caramel-colored hair was mostly twisted up. The hem of her red coat cut precisely across her jean-clad rear, and one end of her polka-dotted scarf fluttered among the loose tendrils of escaped hair as she took quick, decisive steps.

Another version of *Woman Walking Away*.

This was what he would see after he told her the truth, then.

He couldn't do it. He couldn't say the words that would shatter her feelings for him all at once. Those feelings were pure and sincere—yes, they were naive, but they were real, and their destruction could leave a permanent scar. For her own sake, he couldn't sit her down in front of a piece of pie and tell her everything she'd loved about him was a lie. It would break her heart.

It would shatter his.

They emerged from the alley onto a street nearly identical to Main, and then into a mom-and-pop restaurant that smelled of wholesome holiday baking. While gingerbread and pumpkin pie were topped with whipped cream for them, Ryan rapidly formed a new plan.

He didn't want to rip off any damned bandage, so he wouldn't. What if he could reveal pieces of the truth bit by bit, and slowly replace the image of Ryan Michaels with the reality of Ryan Roarke? He'd already told her he worked in California when she'd assumed Montana or Wyoming, and she'd accepted that piece of the truth easily enough. What if he could continue to do that this week? If she loved Ryan Michaels this Sunday, might she love Ryan Roarke by next Sunday?

Could she love him so strongly that she'd still want to be part of his life, even if that life had nothing to do with Montana and her cowgirl dreams?

He had one week to find out.

Chapter Eight

The last thing Kristen needed was more sugar. She was already bouncing off the diner's walls with excitement, because Ryan was here.

He's really here.

Just when she'd given up hope, he'd arrived, and gosh, what a reunion. He'd said everything she could have wanted to hear. He'd missed her. He'd come specifically to see her.

Then there was that kiss on the sidewalk. The memory of kissing Ryan and the reality of kissing Ryan were two entirely different things. Every second had been worth a month of missing him. Everything was okay now. Absolutely everything.

She took her gaze off Ryan just long enough to scoop the whipped cream off the top of her pie and eat it all in one bite, sugar be damned, and then she went back to devouring Ryan with her eyes.

Dear God, he looked good. He was dark-haired and dark-eyed, just like she remembered, and his tan hadn't faded despite the November weather. He still had that air about him that set him apart from the other cowboys in town. Something more sophisticated, maybe. A great haircut, a killer overcoat that even looked good hanging on the wall hook next to hers. The sweater he wore with his jeans almost looked like cashmere. If they ever put a rodeo man on the cover of *GQ*, her Ryan would be the perfect model. He had the strong jaw and an expression that didn't look like he laughed easily—but, oh, when he did, the camera must love him.

A camera. She jumped up to retrieve her phone from her coat's pocket and plopped back into the booth across from Ryan.

"I'm not making the same mistakes this time. Say cheese."

He didn't. Or rather, she didn't give him a chance to say cheese, but she got a wonderful shot of that one raised eyebrow and the quirk of his lips when he was going to smile, but hadn't started actually smiling yet.

She hit the symbols on her phone to make Ryan's image her wallpaper, setting it as her lock screen and home screen, both. "Much better. Sometimes, I was afraid I'd imagined you. Fortunately, the whole town seemed to have seen us sitting on that stage, eating barbecue, so I knew I wasn't crazy." Laughing, she looked up to find him watching her with a too-serious expression.

He laid his hand on the table, palm up, and she gave him her phone. He dialed a number, and within seconds, she heard a traditional, classic ring coming from the coat rack across the room. He disconnected the call and set her phone on the table. She felt relieved, knowing they had each other's numbers now.

"Much better," he said, gently echoing her words. "There was no one around me who knew you existed. I think it did make me a little crazy."

She put her hand in his and squeezed hard.

"I should have come sooner." The regret in his voice was painful to hear.

"You were working." She racked her brain for the California rodeos, information she hadn't thought of since freshman year of high school. "Where were you? Redding? Sacramento?"

"Not Northern California. I'm living in Southern California, believe it or not."

She'd been imagining that he was much closer all this time. It made it all the more understandable that he hadn't been able to steal away for a few days.

Southern California had major rodeos, but as a kid she'd known that she'd never be able to travel that far to see one. Kristen hadn't committed that information to memory, not like the events in Montana and Wyoming. Still, there was something about the serious tone the conversation was taking that made her uneasy. She wanted to keep riding the high of simply being in his presence again.

"Of course I believe you." This time, she winked at him. "It explains the tan."

That seemed to be the right thing to say. He relaxed against the back of his seat. She felt so happy she couldn't stay in hers. She got up and scooted into his side of the booth. His arm came around her immediately, and she snuggled against him like they were teenagers.

She couldn't see every nuance of his facial expressions now, but the trade-off was that her hand could rest on his thigh and her head on his shoulder. He was definitely not a teenager, but a man built for work. Thigh and shoulder, both, were hard-muscled. She was going to want to make love with the lights on.

He tapped her nose with one finger. "Is it the gingerbread or the pumpkin pie that's making you blush?" His voice was low, an intimate rumble for her ears only.

"It's you." She hated the blush, but she couldn't stop the direction her thoughts were going. "I should have guessed you were from Southern California. You don't have a farmer's tan like most of the guys around here."

He was silent for a long moment. "Exactly how do you know that?"

"Let's just say I had an opportunity on the Fourth of July to make use of a certain vantage point."

"Damn. I didn't look down your shirt."

"You're a gentleman. I'm not." She ran one finger down the soft sweater that covered his hard chest. "You're a gentleman who is tan all over. I don't suppose you Southern California cowboys go surfing after the chores are done?"

He shifted slightly. "I do surf, actually."

"You do?" The idea of a surfing cowboy was funny. "Do you wear a cowboy hat out on the waves?"

"Never, and that is the truth." With one finger under her chin, he lifted her face for a sweet kiss.

The diner made a good chaperone. The kiss stayed sweet.

It didn't have to stay sweet, not like the last time Ryan had been in town. She had her own place now. She'd never had a one-night stand. She'd never slept with a man on the first date. But last Fourth of July, she would have made an exception. She might even have blamed it on the punch, thanks to all the buzz in town about its having had a chemical effect in some way, but there was no punch in the picture now, and she wanted Ryan in a fiercely physical way.

Sitting beside him in public and eating a slice of pie set her senses on fire. She'd meant what she'd said on the sidewalk. If she got him alone, she'd seduce him.

He was hers. He'd come back to see her, and he'd come a very long way, too. She wasn't going to make the same mistake twice. If he had to leave the next day, she knew for certain she'd miss him whether they slept together or not, so they might as well—

Leave the next day. Those were chilling words.

"You don't have to fly out in the morning again, do you?"

He brushed her hair out of the way. "I arranged a week off work."

"A whole week. That sounds wonderful." It stretched before her like a huge chunk of time. Seven days. Seven nights.

The nights were on her mind. "Where are you staying while you're here?"

"Maverick Manor."

The name of the place triggered her family pride. "My brother designed that place. Jonah. He's an architect."

"It's one of the most striking hotels I've stayed in."

"Isn't it? It was a private house before he worked on it. I've started working for Jonah myself."

She paused, unsure how to proceed. She had no doubt that she'd know exactly what to do with Ryan if she had him alone in her new bedroom. She'd fantasized about the possibilities in detail, but she'd never considered the first step. How did one let a man know he should take her to her home, come inside and stay the night? She'd always had her parents and brothers under her roof before, so this was a new experience.

"You're working for an architect? That's got to be a huge change. I always imagine you working on your family's ranch."

"I still work there, too, four days a week. I couldn't leave my parents shorthanded." She tapped the edge of her pie plate with her fork. "It also gives me a chance to raid the kitchen and eat some of my mother's home cooking after I'm done in the stables."

"Do you mean you moved off your ranch?" He sounded absolutely stunned.

"I'm living in town. Jonah is renovating a block of gorgeous old Victorian houses. I'm living in one of them and working at the same time, a sort of sweat equity. Instead of paying my rent in cash, I'm paying it by doing some of the renovations. Are you going to eat your whipped cream?"

When he slid his plate toward her, she helped herself.

"To be honest, 'renovating' means I varnish stuff. There's lots and lots of varnishing to be done in a vintage Victorian. Lotsa wood in those babies, and Jonah is crazy about keeping every last piece of original trim. It's all curlicue gingerbread and a real pain in the neck. Pretty to look at, but trust me, you don't want to maintain it."

Ryan was listening to every word she said, and judging by that almost-curve of his mouth and the way his eyes were crinkling a bit at the corners, he liked listening to her. Kristen found that to be a total turn-on that had nothing to do with tanned chests and wash-board abs.

"Do you miss living on the ranch?"

"I probably would if I wasn't still showing up for breakfast four days a week. That's just enough to keep me from being so homesick that I want to move back in. I do miss Kayla, but it's fun to have her popping in for some sister time."

"Congratulations, then, on your first home."

Kristen sat sideways in the booth, tucking one leg under her so she could face him more squarely. "Thank you. Not just for saying that, but for being a big part of the reason I made a lot of changes this fall. Do you remember when we talked about the pursuit of happiness? You said you could be happier, that your work wasn't as rewarding as it had been, and I was so impressed that you were taking action to change things that weren't making you happy."

She hesitated at his slight frown. It probably wasn't realistic to expect him to remember every word they'd said, or even every topic they'd covered throughout the course of that day. She knew every word by heart, but that probably made her look like a lovesick little cow-girl. She wanted him to think of her as so much more.

Still frowning, he reached for one of her wayward curls and wrapped it around his finger. "I remember. Go ahead."

"You inspired me. I realized I was drifting along in a safe routine, but I hadn't stopped to examine what I really wanted. I don't know if you remember that I'd interviewed with the principal—"

"Every word, Kristen. I remember."

Her heart thudded hard, one solid thud, and she knew

it was the sound of a heart falling harder in love. "I decided that just because he'd said no, that didn't mean I had to wait on the ranch for an opportunity to open up. Now I've got my own house, and that was just the beginning."

"That's huge. There's more?"

There was the play, of course. He'd be so proud to know she was using her theater degree. But he was going to be here a full week, and that meant he'd be here on opening night. She was dying to brag about her return to the theater, but this could be a chance to really surprise him on Friday. If she could get him in the audience and then surprise him by appearing on stage, it would be dramatic.

She drew her knee up and hugged it with one arm, still facing him on the bench of the booth. "There might be one or two more things, but you can't expect a woman to divulge every secret at once. I might need to keep a little air of mystery about me."

He raised one eyebrow. "Considering I failed to tell you where I lived, I'm in no position to demand to know all your secrets."

"Here's the important part." She took a deep breath, focused and prepared to deliver her most important line. "You don't need to stay at Maverick Manor this week. I'd like to extend a formal invitation. Mr. Ryan Michaels, would you like to be my first guest in my first home?"

Of all the reactions she might have expected, the way he closed his eyes and turned his face away was not one. Her heart thudded into the silence.

"What's wrong?" she whispered.

The hand he'd rested on the table clenched into a fist. "For one thing, Ryan Michaels is not my name."

"More coffee, you two?"

The owner of the diner had apparently run out of things to do and had come over to chat, interrupting at the worst moment. Ryan needed to explain his name to Kristen. He couldn't sleep with a woman who didn't know his last name, no matter how important she was to him, and he couldn't explain the name confusion if this shop owner didn't leave them alone.

The woman gestured to the phone on the table. "Do you want me to take a picture?" She wiped her free hand on her apron in preparation.

"No, thank you." His curt tone made it clear that she should leave. It would have worked on any server in any city from Los Angeles to London.

Not this woman. She studied him more closely, looking him over. "I haven't seen you in here before. Did you come from the airport? Got a layover tonight?"

This was completely, utterly, not her concern. He glared at her, unwilling to give her a single syllable of *no*, but Kristen let go of the knee she'd been hugging and turned to face her. "He's an old friend of mine, Matilda. We were just catching up. Could you give us just a minute? The pumpkin pie was delicious, by the way."

Matilda kept her eye on Ryan, but she picked up the empty pie plate, took her coffeepot and left. For now.

Ryan had no problem dismissing unnecessary persons, but Kristen accomplished the same thing with a smile. His big-city impatience clashed with her small-town friendliness. He felt like a foreigner once more.

She turned all that sweetness on him. "Was she

standing behind me for long? Did she hear what I said to you? My face is turning ten shades of red now, I can feel it."

"She didn't hear anything."

Kristen had just asked him to spend a week in her home and in her bed. He'd told her she didn't even know his real name, yet she didn't seem hurt or suspicious. He didn't deserve her smile.

"Matilda brought up a good point, though. Did you just fly in today?"

"I landed last night." He hoped his expression was as neutral as he kept it during a trial. He was going to be forced to admit this meeting was a complete accident.

"And you came to Kalispell to find me today, which is…well, not so odd, I guess. Did you stop by the ranch? Maybe Kayla told you I'd be here today."

"No. I just came here because…" There was no hiding the truth in this case. "I had no idea what to say to you when I found you. I came here to walk, basically, and think. Then I planned to head to Rust Creek Falls to find you."

"So it was a total coincidence that you were on the same sidewalk at the same time?"

"It didn't seem so coincidental. I flew in to see you and I was thinking about you when I saw you, but it—"

"—is totally romantic, like you had a sixth sense where I'd be. I've got goose bumps."

Ryan couldn't help it; he had to grin at her relentless optimism. "I was going to say it was totally random."

"Seems more like destiny to me."

That word again. He wasn't ready to claim a belief in destiny, but it seemed better than dwelling on how nervous he'd been to see her again.

Kristen, completely at ease with the situation, helped herself to a bite of his gingerbread. "So, is Ryan Michaels like a stage name? You use it professionally?"

Back to the rodeo, then. She was too trusting. He wished he deserved that trust.

"When we met, I only told you my name was Ryan. It was intentional. I didn't want everyone in town to know who I was."

"You said Michaels much later that night, on the church steps."

"I was talking about the three-year-old version of me. Ryan Michaels was my birth name. It changed when I was adopted."

"Oh, of course. I'm sorry, I didn't think of that."

"Don't apologize. Please."

He had to tell her his real name now. It was the obvious thing to say next, but he hesitated. How well did she know everyone in Rust Creek Falls? His sister and cousin lived there. Maggie Roarke, Lissa Roarke. If for some reason Kristen knew their maiden names, then the bandage would be ripped off whether he liked it or not.

If the fates were kind, Kristen would only know his relatives by their married names. Maggie Crawford. Lissa Christensen.

"So what's your real name?" she asked.

He wouldn't have been surprised if his voice cracked like an adolescent. Thankfully, it did not. "My name is Ryan Roarke."

He waited, dreading the next spark of recognition, the inevitable *are you related to...?*

"Roarke," she repeated. "I like it." Then she took a sip of her coffee.

Incredible. Wonderful. He'd dodged the bullet. She didn't know Maggie and Lissa's maiden names.

Thankfully, neither his sister nor cousin had any business on the Dalton's family ranch, and he doubted Kristen had ever needed legal help from Maggie Crawford or hung out in the sheriff's office where Lissa Christensen's photo might have been on the sheriff's desk. His cowgirl wasn't the type to track down everyone's backgrounds—not like the owner of this diner—and for that, he was grateful.

"Ryan Roarke. It's a little catchier than Ryan Michaels, with the two *R*'s. Do a lot of rodeo performers use stage names?"

"I have no idea. Roarke is my real name." He felt the flash of guilt, although he was telling the truth. He *didn't* know if rodeo stars used stage names, although it seemed likely some would.

"It certainly explains why I didn't find you when I typed 'Ryan Michaels rodeo' in my internet search." She put her head back on his shoulder, and Ryan closed his eyes in both guilt and relief.

If she assumed he was still a rodeo star, well…they were getting closer to the truth. Bit by bit. Slow and steady, so that nothing would abruptly shatter beyond repair.

In his mind's eye, he saw the snow globe hit the church steps.

He opened his eyes, took in the sight of Kristen curved against him, the soft leather of the booth's high-backed bench sheltering them both. Nothing harsh. Nothing hard.

Beyond their booth, outside the wide glass panes of the storefront window, snow started falling in slow, fluffy flakes. He had the fleeting thought that he was inside the snow globe.

He hugged Kristen to him tightly. He didn't want anything to break. Not this time.

"That coffee has got to be cold by now." The woman in the apron reappeared, holding her coffeepot above their cooled cups, poised for action if he'd just say the word. "You might as well have it warm."

Ryan curtly nodded his permission.

Too harsh. Too hard.

He mustered up a smile as she poured the hot coffee. "Thank you. Everything here is warm. It's a nice place."

"Well." She produced a fresh spoon from her apron pocket and set it in front of Kristen. "Well, you just stay here and enjoy. It's only going to get colder out there."

"Oh, man," Kristen said in a stage whisper. "Somebody's going to get extra whipped cream from now on."

"I heard you," Matilda said over her shoulder. "You and your old friend just remember that we make wedding cakes here, too."

Chapter Nine

Ryan took her to dinner.

Kristen took him home.

Impatient with the slow burn of sexual tension that had been building all day, Kristen led the way back to Rust Creek Falls in her compact SUV and parallel parked on the street of vintage houses. She waited on the sidewalk while Ryan pulled his rented truck into the next closest spot. Her mind was still processing the incredible fact that today was the day that Ryan Michaels had come back.

No, it was Roarke. Ryan Roarke had come back.

But while her heart and mind kept feeling surprised—*today!*—her body was already well beyond that acceptance phase. Every inch of her craved the intimacy which every smoldering look over a candlelit dinner in Kalispell had promised. They were adults who wanted each other, who'd wanted each other since a waltz in July, and the time had come.

Ryan kept his hands in the pockets of his overcoat as he walked up to her, looking sexy and self-contained. Kristen felt a little shiver of nervous awareness. She might be an adult, but six feet of confident, controlled male wasn't something she invited into her bedroom. Ever. Her past lovers, which numbered exactly two, might as well have never existed, for all that her experience with them had prepared her for a night with this man. Ryan Roarke was in a league of his own.

"Which house is yours?" The bass in his voice struck just the right, delicious note.

She wanted this. Him. Them. So she lifted her chin with a confidence she didn't quite possess and held up her phone, acting as if she weren't dying to get him in the door and naked on the floor. "I'll give you a clue. I told you Jonah was a fanatic about keeping all the original wood. He doesn't feel that way about the electrical wiring. He's completely in love with high tech in his buildings. Ready?"

She punched a code into her phone, and like magic, the second house from the corner lit up. A rainbow of multicolored Christmas lights delineated the elegant lines of its arched front porch. "Isn't it wonderful?"

Ryan shook his head in amusement. "It's not even Thanksgiving yet."

"Less than two weeks away. Come with me. I have to light up the best thing myself."

She slid her phone into her pocket as she led the way up the newly installed wood stairs. Just last week, she'd sealed them against the coming winter weather. Today's flurries were already gone, but she had the satisfaction of knowing the wood had been protected against them.

On the wide porch, Kristen plugged an extension cord into an outlet near the front door. "Ta-da!"

Ryan turned to look at her most treasured garage sale find: a molded plastic Santa that was four feet tall and lit up from the inside by an old-fashioned, sixty-watt light bulb.

"Isn't he great? He should be in the yard, but I'm keeping him on the porch to protect him from the elements. He's the real deal from 1968."

Ryan had gone very quiet beside her, hands still in his pockets.

"He needs a Mrs. Claus, of course. He's half of a pair—you know, the kind where Mr. and Mrs. Claus are leaning forward to kiss each other?"

Ryan stepped behind her, very close.

"It's going to be a challenge to find her, but I've got alerts set on eBay."

Ryan pulled up the bottom edge of her coat and set his hands on her hips, his fingertips grazing her middle as he held her firmly to him. The street was empty, but her winter coat would have made it hard for anyone to see exactly what he was doing.

"Until I find a vintage Mrs. Claus, Santa will just have to blow kisses to the people on the sidewalk, even though I don't have any neighbors yet. Oh, Lord, I'm babbling, aren't I?"

Ryan bent to kiss her neck, nudging her scarf out of the way with his chin, replacing the material's warmth with the warmth of his mouth as he tasted the soft skin under her jaw. As her knees turned to jelly, he slid one hand across her stomach, wrapping his arm around her waist for support.

"My keys," she said, sounding as breathy as a vintage movie star. "Let me just…" She patted her pocket, felt her phone, pulled out her house keys.

Ryan turned her in his arms and kissed her full-on, capturing her gasp in that zero-to-sixty escalation of passion that she didn't want to slow down. He moved them farther away from the row of colored lights, pressing her back against the door's deep framing as he kissed her senseless, or nearly senseless. She kept just enough brain power going to fit the key in the lock and turn it.

She fumbled for the antique iron doorknob but his hand covered hers, his breath hot against her lips, his body hard against hers. "I'm not coming in," he murmured between tastes of her.

"You're—*what*?"

"Not tonight. I'm not coming in." Then he kissed her, hungry, making love to her mouth the way she wanted his body to make love to hers.

"Come in," she gasped. "Now. Please."

With a sharp sound of frustration, he jerked her coat up a little farther. Cold air chased his hot hand as he slid from her belly to her lacy, thin bra. He cupped one whole breast, shaping her softness to the contours of his hand. She melted at his touch, sliding down the frame an inch, grasping with her free hand for an anchor until she clutched his coat's lapel for support.

She tried to say *yes, more, don't stop*, but only whimpered deep in her throat. He stopped caressing her, and they stayed locked in that embrace, not moving, not kissing, just breathing.

"This is a bad idea," he said, panting in a way that made Kristen feel incredibly desirable.

"This is a great idea." She pressed her head back against the framing so that she could look him in the eye. "This is...powerful."

He sharpened his gaze, losing a little of that sexual haze. She knew he remembered using that word when they'd kissed in the summer.

"So come into the house."

"What's between you and me is not going to disappear," he said. "It will be powerful tomorrow, and the day after that, and after that."

Darn the man for using her own summer words against her.

He withdrew his hand and tugged her coat down. He still had her crowded against the door, but she felt that he was creating a deliberate distance all the same.

"If this feeling isn't going to change, then why not tonight?" Her hand jerked his lapel with her plea, a tiny motion that betrayed her huge frustration. They were so, so close.

He kissed her pouting lower lip, soothing her. Placating her.

She didn't want that. She wanted him, so she let go of the doorknob to grab his other lapel and pulled him to her with both fists. Her kiss wasn't soothing. It went from zero to sixty for both of them.

"Because," he said, a long minute later.

It took her a second to realize he was answering her question.

"Not tonight, because you don't know me. Not well enough for this."

"That's crazy. You're all I've thought about for four

months. I didn't believe in love at first sight, until I met you."

After a long moment, Ryan bowed his head. He nodded, even as he turned from her and took a step away, putting real physical distance between them.

She'd put the word out there. *Love.*

Her heart thudded, hard.

"Until a few hours ago, that love at first sight was for a rodeo star named Ryan Michaels. That's not me." His voice sounded harsh. The look in his eyes was...hurt.

So, he must have left the rodeo, something that had been a huge part of his life. He was no longer a rodeo star, and it bothered him. She didn't know how to help a man leave a career behind. To make it worse, she'd called him by the wrong name today, a name that reminded him of the worst time of his life. That, at least, she could fix.

"Your last name doesn't change my feelings. Ryan Michaels grew into the man Ryan Roarke is. You've been you all along."

He looked at her across three feet of porch planking as if he were looking at a woman who was far out of his reach. "Trust me on this. You should know me better before we make love. I do mean make love, because as powerful and crazy as this is, it's real. It would gut me if we made love and you came to regret it."

But there is a chance you might.

The implication was clear. So was Ryan's expression, his stance. Everything about him as he warned her off seemed straightforward and sincere.

What could she learn about him that would possibly cause her to regret having slept with him? She didn't regret sleeping with her college sweetheart, even though the relationship hadn't lasted. Then there was Captain Two-Timer—

She regretted that one. Ryan was right; there were a few possibilities that would be showstoppers for her.

"Okay, then. In the interest of avoiding any future regret, can I ask you a few questions?"

"Yes."

"Are you married?"

Surprise flickered across his face. "No."

"Involved with another woman? Is there another woman in another small town who thinks you arc coming back for her?"

"No. I'm not using you to cheat on anyone else. It goes without saying that I'd never cheat on you."

"It goes without saying." She still felt like a fool for not having realized the truth about her pilot sooner. "But it's still better to have that one laid out as a ground rule."

"It sounds like there's a man out there, somewhere, who'd be better off not crossing your path again. Or mine." He crossed the gap he'd put between them, and brushed a few loose strands of hair away from her cheek. His fingers were cool in the night air. "No other women. An easy promise, one I've been keeping since the day I met you."

She shivered at his touch and his words, and let her eyes close.

Kiss me, kiss me.

He put his hand back in his pocket. "Did you have any other questions?"

She opened her eyes, disappointed. What else could cause her to regret sleeping with Ryan Roarke, whom she'd dreamed about for months, who'd traveled the length of the country just to see her again? "Do you have a disease?"

"Fair question. No. Do you?"

"Oh, you mean…no, not those kind of diseases. I mean, I've got nothing, uh, contagious. That wasn't what I was asking—but we should be asking, of course, I just wasn't, and…" She could beg him to make love to her without blushing, but everything else seemed to make her cheeks burn.

She took a deeper breath. "I meant, are you dying of any disease? Am I going to regret making love to you when I find out you have an inoperable brain tumor or something? Not that I wouldn't still care for you, though. If our time is short, I'd want to make love to you all the more, really."

"I see." His lips twitched into that almost-curve. "Nothing that I know of."

"Don't laugh at me. It would be horrible. Those are my least favorite movies. You can't drag me into a theater to watch heartbreak like that."

She was glad to see his sense of humor returning, anyway, his expression relaxing into a smile, although he maintained his stiff posture, hands in his pockets. As his chuckle made his breath puff out in little white clouds, it occurred to her that he might be cold. They'd had some flurries today, and he was used to the weather in Southern California, not at the Canadian border.

"We could go inside to talk. It's pretty cold out here. I promise not to seduce you."

"I can't make the same promise. Every minute we talk makes you more appealing."

She wrinkled her nose. "What turned you on? The talk about diseases or my sorry history of being cheated on?"

"It was the way you made yourself blush, and the way your past experience makes me feel so protective of your heart."

Thud. The man could stop her heart with his words.

She threw up her hands in frustration. "You know, Ryan, if you're going to talk like that, you have to take me to bed."

He smiled a bit, but he had those sad eyes again. "Let's give it a little time. Are there any other showstoppers you'd like to ask before I admit that I'm freezing and say good-night?"

"Showstoppers. That's exactly the word I was thinking. We're so alike." She looked around at her Christmas lights and her plastic Santa. "I'm drawing a blank here. I can't imagine what you're afraid I'll find out about you. Unless…"

"Unless?"

"You don't have any sexual fetishes I should know about? You're not into, like, Roman orgy reenactments or anything?"

Ryan crossed his arms over his chest and leaned one shoulder against the wall. "I'm not that cold, after all. Let's discuss this. Roman orgies are out, then? What other sexual fetishes are off the table? Or on?"

Kristen crossed her arms over her chest and leaned against the wall, too. "Describe yours for me, and I'll decide."

She'd managed to keep a straight face, but Ryan just about doubled over with sudden laughter. She was laughing, too, when he kissed her softly, then stepped back before she could test his willpower with a more passionate kiss. "On that note, I better leave. I'm already not going to be able to sleep tonight."

"Will I see you tomorrow?"

"What's the earliest possible time I can pick you up?"

It was so lovely to be with a man who was as eager to see her as she was to see him. "Actually, I have to work tomorrow at the Circle D. I'll be there by six."

"In the morning?"

"Of course. Why don't you come? You could check out our horses. I've got one who's an absolute nightmare to get trailered. You must know tons of good tricks about transporting animals."

Ryan's smile faded.

"Or maybe that's a really dumb idea. I'm sorry, I forgot this is your vacation. You probably don't want to muck out a stall on vacation."

He rubbed his jaw, then nodded as if he'd come to a decision. "The Circle D is a part of who you are. I'd like to see it. I'll pick you up and we can drive to the ranch together."

"Actually, if we showed up in the same rig before sunrise, my family might jump to some conclusions about how we'd spent the night. I wouldn't mind doing the time if I'd done the crime, so to speak, but why don't you just meet me there? Anytime after six will be fine."

"All right. I'm looking forward to seeing a genuine cowgirl in her natural habitat."

"Whatever you say, cowboy."

Ryan's smile didn't touch those sad eyes as he left without risking another kiss.

A *cowboy*.

Ryan threw his coat on the log bed of his hotel room. Throwing a well-tailored length of blended wool was a completely unsatisfying outlet for his frustration. A punching bag or a sparring session in the boxing ring would be better. Instead, he had to prepare to spend tomorrow with a bunch of horses.

He didn't know squat about horses, but Kristen was going to expect him to give her advice. She'd talked about love at first sight tonight, but she'd meant love at the first sight of a cowboy.

He was no horse whisperer, but his brother-in-law was. Ryan called Jesse.

Maggie answered, of course. Being both a lawyer and his sister, she was doubly direct.

"Did you straighten things out with Kristen?"

Ryan yanked off one boot. "I'm working on it, Maggie. Let me talk to Jesse."

"Working on it? You didn't tell her the truth?"

"We're getting there. She knows I live in Southern California now. She knows my name is Roarke."

"Roarke the rodeo star? Or Roarke the attorney?"

"Let me talk to Jesse."

"You've got to tell her. The longer you let this go on, the more hurt she's going to be when she finds out the truth."

He yanked off the other boot. "I never told her I was a rodeo star."

"But you're letting her believe it. She's going to hate you for that when she finds out the truth."

She's going to hate you...

He couldn't stand the thought. He hated the very words. God, he wanted only for her to love him.

"Ryan?"

He set the boot down carefully, lining it up neatly beside the rough-hewn leg of the rustic chair.

"Ask Jesse to call me when he gets a chance." His

voice sounded calm. His hand was steady when he tapped the button to end the call.

She's going to hate you...

He dropped his head in his hands and gave in to the shudder that racked his body.

Tonight, she'd said she loved him—or, at least, that she believed it was possible to have fallen in love with him at first sight. She didn't seem to resent him for being gone for months, and so far, she wasn't upset that at least two of her assumptions about him had been wrong. A name and a home state, those she could forgive—because she loved him?

Love should be unchangeable. He should be able to tell Kristen everything: Ryan Michaels, Ryan Roarke, cowboy, attorney. None of it should matter, but he had an old Christmas memory that proved otherwise.

Love was not unconditional, no matter what fairy tales others believed. A mother could decide she didn't love a little boy anymore. Nothing good lasted forever. He had to be careful with Kristen, and handle the possibility that she loved him with care.

He had a good plan. Kristen had pieced together one picture of him, and he was going to replace the wrong pieces, one at a time. Some day, Kristen might think his skills in a courtroom were impressive, but tomorrow, he'd be in a stable. He didn't want to look like an ass. When the phone rang, he knew what he had to do.

"Jesse. I've got a hypothetical situation for you. It's six in the morning, and you walk into a stable full of horses. What's the first thing you do?"

Chapter Ten

Ryan entered the stables with trepidation.

His brother-in-law had said the first thing he did was walk the entire length of the barn, once through. "You can get a feel right away if the horses as a group are calm. Then I look for any one horse who seems out of sorts."

According to Jesse, every barn had its own feed and care routine, so Ryan should follow Kristen's lead and respect the routine of the Circle D—as if Ryan might have a different routine in mind.

"You don't need special training to dump feed into a bucket or skim loose hay out of a water trough," Jesse had said.

"If she asks me to do anything more complex than that, what's your advice for a man who last touched a horse at eighth-grade summer camp?"

Jesse had laughed. "Generally speaking, horses are

patient creatures. They'll put up with a lot when they know you're trying."

"Generally speaking?"

"Good luck."

Ryan's first step into the barn startled a cat that bolted across his path and headed up a pile of hay bales to the safety of the rafters.

"I know how you feel," Ryan said under his breath. He wished he could dodge potential danger as effectively, but helping Kristen with her morning chores was a minefield he had to negotiate. He'd considered changing their plans. He could pick her up once she'd returned to her house and take her out for a nice lunch. Dinner and a movie. But he couldn't sleep in the plush bedding at Maverick Manor knowing Kristen was working hard in the cold November dawn. It offended some sense of chivalry or manhood deep down, concepts that were probably outdated, but he felt them nonetheless.

His first sight of Kristen Dalton in her natural element forced him to be more honest with himself. She looked like his most cherished Montana fantasy come true. This wasn't about helping a damsel in distress; this was about spending every possible moment with this woman, period. Full stop. If Kristen wanted to be with him, he wanted to be with her, wherever, whenever and doing whatever.

Her back was to him as she hung a pitchfork on a wall hook. Despite the barn's temperature being nearly the same as outside, Kristen wore only a faded pink sweatshirt and blue jeans. Her glorious hair, something that could easily become a fetish of his, hung in one long braid down her back, bouncing with each step as she pushed a wheelbarrow away from him, heading for the open door at the opposite end of the barn.

"Just cool your jets, tough guy. I'll get to you in a minute."

Ryan stopped in surprise, until a black horse stuck its head out of the stall she'd just passed and snorted at her, shaking its mane impatiently. Kristen continued out the wide door without stopping.

Ryan slowly walked down the center aisle of the barn, absorbing the feel of the place. It was spacious and organized, and smelled equally of animals and hay. Most of the stalls were empty, so he assumed they normally held the horses that he'd seen milling about in a fenced-in grassy area adjacent to the barn. As Ryan reached the door through which Kristen had taken her wheelbarrow, the black horse and three others stuck their massive heads over their half doors and looked at him with knowing, dark eyes.

He wondered if he should have brought carrots or some other bribe. He held his palm up to the brown beauty closest to him. "Sorry, I've got nothing."

The horse snuffled his palm, anyway. He petted its nose, the softness as surprising now as it had been in eighth grade. Ryan moved to the next stall and repeated the greeting with the next horse. He could see what Jesse had meant about being able to get a feel for the horses' attitude. Ryan could tell these animals were content and cared for. It didn't take a lifetime of ranch experience to recognize good health and a friendly disposition.

The black horse across the aisle bit at his door's latch and bobbed his head in a demanding way. The name plate over his stall identified him as Zorro. "Everyone's patient except you, son. You need to work on your attitude. You heard Kristen. Don't rush the woman."

"That's right, Zorro. I hope you're paying attention." Kristen's voice had a laugh in it. She let go of her empty wheelbarrow and came toward Ryan with her arms open for a hug, but she stopped short. "You look too nice. I'll get you all dirty."

Ryan took the final step toward her and scooped her against him. "You look fantastic."

"Oh, yes. Like a mucker of stalls."

"The braid and boots thing is definitely working for me." He lingered for a few dangerous seconds longer than he should have as he kissed the happy curve of her mouth, and set her down again.

"If braids and boots are your fetish, you'll be in heaven here in Rust Creek Falls. Put it in your plus column."

He couldn't resist touching the fine bones of her face, trailing his fingers over her cheekbone and along her jawline. Such delicate features for a woman as strong as she was. "The braid and boots only turn me on when your pretty face is part of the package."

Her gaze flickered over his shoulder. "I told you that you'd be in heaven. There are two women in Rust Creek Falls who meet your criteria."

Ryan turned to see a duplicate of Kristen walking toward them. It was disconcerting for a second, like seeing a special effect from a movie, although he'd known she had an identical twin. On the Fourth of July, they'd passed her sister a few times on the dance floor, but there'd been clear differences in their clothing and hair and the way they moved. Now, in jeans and boots and the braid he supposed was practical for working in a barn, they were startlingly identical.

"You must be Kayla," he said, extending his hand.

She dropped her gaze but took his hand, then looked up at him again with a shy duck of her chin. She was so unlike Kristen in her actions Ryan doubted he'd ever be fooled for more than a second.

"And you must be Ryan Michaels." Her voice was quiet in the cavernous barn.

Kristen jumped in. "It's Ryan Roarke, actually. My mistake. That's why I couldn't find him in any rodeo results."

"Roarke?" Kayla looked at him more directly. "Are you related to Lissa Roarke, then?"

Ryan released her hand, but not before she must have felt his little jolt of surprise. She knew maiden names, obviously. This was an unexpected mine that needed to be carefully defused.

"Lissa who?" Kristen asked.

"Lissa Christensen," her sister explained patiently. "The sheriff's wife. She was Lissa Roarke when she came here from New York and wrote that blog about the flood, remember?"

"Oh." Kristen turned to him and made a little gesture toward her sister. "If it has to do with writing or newspapers, she's into it. English major."

Ryan smiled, ignoring his racing heart. "Lissa is my cousin. She grew up in New York, though, while I was in…"

"California," Kristen finished for him, and she turned to her sister. "He's from California."

Ryan knew instinctively that Kristen was anxious to prove that she knew him well, although she hadn't made the connection with Lissa.

"Is that why you were here for the Fourth of July, then?" Kristen asked, phrasing her question like her sister. "You were visiting Lissa? That makes so much sense."

"Lissa was in New York because Gage was on duty for the whole holiday weekend." Ryan hadn't lied about his intention that day in the park, and he wasn't going to start now. "I came to look into relocating to Rust Creek Falls, remember?"

Kristen's expression brightened. "But now I know how you heard of Rust Creek Falls in the first place. A cousin has to go in the plus column. Being far from your parents is a bigger minus, but at least you'll have some family in town."

She was still so certain that the plus column would win. Whether or not Lissa lived in town didn't change the fact that the full responsibility for Roarke and Associates was being laid on his shoulders by his parents' impending retirement. Once he explained the situation fully, he hoped Kristen would understand. The dream he'd toyed with in July about living here couldn't become a reality. They'd have to be a long-distance couple, or she'd have to move to LA.

The black horse chose that moment to remind them all that he was not where he wanted to be.

"Okay, Zorro. Chill out. Let me check your feet before I turn you out." With efficient movements and a grace that Ryan was certain could only come from a lifetime of working with horses, Kristen put a halter on the black horse and led him out of his stall, then tied him to a railing in the aisle with some kind of knot that Ryan had probably failed at tying back in his scouting days. She grabbed a small tool from a bucket that hung on the wall, and crouched down to lift the massive animal's front hoof. With a series of soothing "good boys," she started working on Zorro's hoof.

Kayla picked up the handles of the wheelbarrow. "I'll be mucking stalls if you need me."

"I'll help." Ryan was confident he could master a pitchfork faster than the two-step, and he'd mastered that in less than one verse of a country-western song.

"You'll ruin your clothes," Kayla said. "That overcoat is just too nice for chores."

"It's all I brought on this trip. It can be cleaned."

Kristen looked up from her crouch on the floor. "Just put on another coat. I think Eli left that one here." She pointed with her pick to a beige canvas coat that hung on a wall with a cluster of leather straps and ropes.

Ryan hung his long overcoat in its place. The battered canvas coat was the same temperature as the crisp November air that filled the barn from the open doors. He'd barely shrugged into it when gentle Kayla took another tool out of the bucket and lobbed it not so gently at Ryan. He caught it by the wood handle, thankfully, because the rest of it looked like a loop made from a metal saw.

"Zorro has sensitive feet. If you brush him at the same time, he won't be so fussy for Kristen." She took the wheelbarrow and headed down the aisle to an empty stall.

Ryan thought the tool in his hand looked more likely to torture than soothe. He walked up to the horse, struck anew at just how large the beast was. He scraped the teeth of the metal loop lightly along Zorro's side. The horse didn't object, so he did it again, a little more firmly.

Kristen moved to the other front hoof, so Ryan kept running the brush along the horse, resting his free hand on the horse's neck as he worked, appreciating the heat and power contained in the muscles under the black coat. Although Zorro's hair had seemed to be too short to be brushed, the shades of black varied after each stroke as the nap of the hair reflected light at a new angle. Ryan kept the brush moving in a methodical pattern over the black gloss.

"I can see why he finds this soothing." Immediately, Ryan realized he'd said something that revealed this was a new experience for him. *Too soon, don't shatter—* but he couldn't cover the mistake without lying, and he couldn't lie to Kristen.

"Zorro's one of those that really love it. Of course, Snoopy over there really hates it. You know how it is. What works with one horse has the opposite effect on another." She moved to another hoof. "Good boy. You boys like to keep us guessing, don't you, Zorro?"

Ryan relaxed again. The sky outside the double doors began to lighten with the coming dawn. Incredibly, despite his blunder, Kristen assumed he knew horses. Then again, growing up on a ranch in Montana, maybe a person who *didn't* know horses was as foreign to her as an alien from a UFO.

He chose his words with care. "Kristen, I never told you I was in the rodeo. What makes you think I am?"

She stood up, finished with that hoof, and looked at him over Zorro's back. She rested her arm on the horse as she talked, like one would lean on a piece of furniture. She was completely comfortable around an animal that weighed one thousand pounds. Her unconscious confidence was sexy.

"Every once in a while, someone at the picnic would recognize you. I knew right away that you couldn't be just another hand making the rounds of the ranches, looking for work. You carry yourself like you are used to being in charge. Besides, and please don't think I'm materialistic or anything, you don't dress like the average ranch hand. You must be doing something that's a little more lucrative than a standard cowboy paycheck. I put two and two together."

She disappeared again, crouching down to pick up the last hoof.

Ryan kept brushing. It had been that simple, then. For a woman who only knew cowboys, there was only one kind of cowboy who would get recognized at the town picnic.

"Have you ever *not* dated a cowboy?"

The scraping sounds stopped for a moment.

"Once."

The scraping started again.

"He was from the city."

She said the word *city* like it was a curse. She referred to Kalispell as a city, with its population of how many? Twenty thousand? Los Angeles was a city of fifteen or sixteen million. If she thought a place like Kalispell was too big, she'd hate Ryan Roarke's reality.

"He was based in Denver."

A bigger city, then, but still small compared to Ryan's.

"A pilot."

The bitterness in that simple word snapped his attention from his own sorry worries back to Kristen. Bitterness was rare from her, but he'd heard it once before, during last night's conversation on the porch. Her one experience with a non-cowboy had been a bad one.

Ryan worked his way around to her side of the horse, brushing as he went, staying calm. "This was the guy who didn't understand that some things go without saying."

In her crouched position, her head was bowed, and her hands went still. "He was in the shower, getting ready to go back to work after his layover. His phone was right next to me on the nightstand. The screen lit up that he'd gotten a text, with a little preview of the message. There was this tiny thumbnail photo of a topless girl, and the first line said, See you at five. The current time was in big numbers, 10:16. That will be stuck in my brain for a long time."

Zorro threw his head up, objecting to the stroke of the brush. Ryan stopped until the first wave of jealousy and anger passed, then he crouched down next to Kristen.

"I told him off, of course," she said. "He put on his uniform and left me in the hotel. Seven hours after we'd been in bed together, I knew he was back in Denver, having sex with her. Breaking up with me didn't hurt him for half a day. I'm sure I was just some dumb cowgirl from Montana to him. Another variety to add to his menu."

Ryan kept his fury at the unknown pilot under control, mindful of his tone of voice around the horse. "I know that type. He'll never be faithful to anyone, ever, and it doesn't matter how wonderful the woman is."

It was rare for Kristen not to look him in the eye, but she toyed with the pick in her hand for a moment, then ran her hand down Zorro's leg, soothing the horse to soothe herself.

"Believe me, Kristen. It wasn't that you weren't a good enough girlfriend. The fault is all his."

She nodded. "I get that. I do. It's just that I'm ashamed of myself for believing his lies. I should have been able to see through them. I saw him every other week, and never questioned what he did or who he did it with between those times. He looked me right in the eye and lied to me, over and over, trip after trip."

She's going to hate you when she finds out the truth.

He couldn't tell her about himself today. He couldn't risk it. At that moment, he wanted, more than anything else in the world, to be a cowboy for Kristen, so she'd never doubt her own judgment again.

"I made a promise to myself," she said. "No more city slickers. I wished for a cowboy, and now here you are."

With regret, with tenderness, Ryan kissed her cheek. He hadn't lied, but he hadn't told her the complete truth. He stayed crouched beside her, wanting to tell her something true. "It goes without saying, I am with you and only you."

"I know. Cowboys get it."

"No. *I* get it. It's got nothing to do with cowboys, and everything to do with you. Because you're such an amazing person, there's no room in my head or my heart for another woman."

The wheelbarrow came to a halt beside them. Kayla crouched down. "What is it? Does Zorro have a cracked hoof again?"

Kristen barely glanced at her sister, but apparently, the look was enough between identical twins.

"Never mind." Kayla stood and pushed the wheelbarrow away.

Ryan stood and resumed his brushing, hoping the motion would help him center himself and bring back that calm feeling.

It didn't. It couldn't, because he hadn't clarified anything with Kristen except his desire for her, and she had to have known that already.

Kristen finished with whatever she'd been doing to the horse's feet and started loving on the horse, petting his nose and telling him sweet nothings. "You are being spoiled today, aren't you? Don't get any ideas about leaving me for Ryan. You can't run off to join the rodeo with him. No fame and fortune for you."

"Kristen."

He couldn't do this. He couldn't let her go on believing he was a rodeo star.

Don't risk it. Don't let it shatter.

He couldn't rip the bandage off, but he had to make one point perfectly clear. "My name won't ever be in your newspaper for winning a rodeo event. There will be no tour and no fame and glory. If that's what you're looking for in a relationship, I can't offer it to you."

She left the horse's side to walk up to him in that unhurried way ranchers seemed to move, but he didn't reach for her, nor she for him. They stood in the open door of the barn, the sunrise coloring the sky beyond them, the cold air between them.

"I didn't ask you to." Her blue-eyed gaze was unwavering. "It sounds like you haven't had a great love life in the past, either. Instead of a two-timing pilot, I'm guessing there's a woman who was more interested in getting close to fame than in getting close to you. Probably a lot of women over the years."

Every relationship. Some very intelligent women, some very talented, all of them beautiful and all of them, every single one, hoping to improve her Hollywood clout and connections. The up-and-coming actresses, the aging actresses, the models who wanted to be actresses. The pressure was constant in Hollywood; the game of who knew whom was crucial to landing parts. He didn't blame them, but he was weary. Kristen's complete lack of interest in Hollywood added to her small-town appeal.

"It's a career hazard. I've dated women like that too often."

"Was this what you were afraid I'd regret? That I would be sorry I'd slept with you if you weren't going to be on the rodeo tour next season? Because that would be insulting to me, and it would hurt to think you knew me so little. I realize you're used to women who want to travel with a celebrity, but I'm not that kind of woman."

"I know you're not." She was fresh-faced, makeup free, a naturally beautiful woman against the backdrop of a beautiful part of the country. Her braid had fallen forward and was lying over one breast. He wanted her fiercely. "You are too much a part of this ranch and this town to want to waste your life on the road."

"Well, that sounds nicer than saying I'm a homebody, I guess." Her smile was as irrepressible as the growing sunrise. Ryan wanted to hold her close and feel that warmth.

Reading his mind, she stepped into his willing arms and laid her head on his shoulder. He caught her close and kissed her hair, the corner of her eye, the bridge of her nose. She relaxed under his touch, the change in her muscle tension as obvious as Zorro's had been.

"I'm so glad you're here. After this week, will you be gone long?"

"I'm spending Thanksgiving with my parents. After that…"

He didn't know. He hadn't thought beyond this week, beyond satisfying that burning need he'd had to see Kristen once more, just once more. Standing in this barn, the differences in their lives were more obvious to him than ever.

So was his need to be with her. One week with her would not be enough.

"It may be a while, but…" He shook his head at his own idiocy. He wasn't kidding anyone, least of all himself. "I don't think I can go without you very long. I'll come back."

"I knew that last July." She shushed the impatient Zorro, then turned her sunny smile on Ryan once more. "But it's nice that you know it now, too. Four months was a long time for you to realize you should come back to the place you said makes you feel at peace. I hated knowing you were out there somewhere, not at peace."

"Montana doesn't give me peace. You do."

The sound of a very loud, very human yawn startled them both. Kayla was behind them, stretching her arms overhead as she sat on an overturned barrel. "I hate to bother you two, but if we could turn out these last four horses and clean the stalls…" She yawned again.

Kristen frowned a little. "Another late night? You've been tired a lot lately."

"I'm fine. I'm just trying to live without coffee."

Kristen looked horrified. "No coffee? Why would you do that?"

Kayla ducked her head, shy once more. "Caffeine is supposed to be bad for you. I read this blog that made me want to try going without it. Just for a little while."

"Sis, I love you, but that's nuts. Maybe you should get some breakfast. Ryan's here. He'll help me finish up."

Kayla left after a few more protests. Kristen picked up a pitchfork and sifted through the hay in Zorro's empty stall, coming up with a clump of manure and tossing it into the wheelbarrow. "Why don't you turn out the rest of the horses while I get started on the dirty work?"

Ryan took one look at the ropes and knots and bridles hanging on the wall and took the pitchfork out of Kristen's hands. "I'm sure your horses would rather say good morning to you." He was also certain he'd make a fool of himself trying to put a bridle on a horse for the first time. A pitchfork took no skill, only muscle, and that, thankfully, he had.

Kristen slipped a leather bridle around the brown horse's head, reaching up to guide its ears under a strap, all while keeping her gaze on Ryan. "We can get breakfast afterward."

Ryan stopped in midscoop. Here was another obstacle he hadn't planned on negotiating. If he met her parents, there would be the inevitable getting-to-know-you questions. He tossed the manure into the wheelbarrow. "I hadn't planned on meeting your parents this morning."

Before he could add an acceptable excuse, Kristen jumped in. "Oh, I didn't mean breakfast at the house.

It was too late last night to call and tell them you'd be here this morning. I know my mom. She'd kill me if I walked into the kitchen with you while she was in her bathrobe."

Kristen led Zorro and the brown horse around the wheelbarrow, stopping in front of him and tossing her braid back over her shoulder with a graceful movement of her head and shoulder. "My house in town is always an option."

Her hands were full and so were his, but their mouths met with a hunger that had nothing to do with breakfast.

"Wow. You weren't kidding about the braids and boots, were you?"

"Your house is not a safe option." He stepped back. "How about that donut shop from our tour?"

"Bear claws and coffee. Sounds perfect."

"Go Grizzlies."

"Spoken like a true Rust Creek Falls native."

He had no answer for that, either, as Kristen led the two horses out of the barn.

He wasn't a native, and no matter how content he felt in Montana, he couldn't leave his parents and their practice. It was clear that Kristen belonged here with her family just as strongly. He couldn't pull this sweet cowgirl out of Montana, and he couldn't hide from his responsibilities in California, either.

He jabbed the pitchfork into the hay. He'd be lucky to get away from work one weekend every few months. Her two-timing pilot had been able to spend more time with her than Ryan could. How long would he and Kristen keep these tender emotions and this burning attraction going? Through how many lonely months of separation between the occasional three-day weekend?

He dumped more waste into the wheelbarrow.

Nothing good lasted forever.

It couldn't be done.

Ryan stared at his laptop in defeat. The firm's calendar was no more flexible than a judge's gavel. There was no way Ryan could squeeze in a return visit to Montana between Thanksgiving and Christmas. When he left Kristen at the end of the week, he'd be leaving her until February, at the very earliest.

I'm in love with you, Kristen. I'll miss Thanksgiving, Christmas and New Year's, but I can make it back by Groundhog Day, and Memorial Day three months after that. Is that the relationship with a cowboy you've always dreamed of?

His reality sucked. He needed to tell her all of it, before someone else burst their private bubble. If he kept taking Kristen on dates in Rust Creek Falls, it was inevitable they'd run into Brad Crawford or Lissa or, God forbid, Maggie.

Disaster had been narrowly avoided this morning. After they'd mucked the last stalls and washed up, they'd headed for the donut shop. As Ryan had rounded the corner in his rented rig, the local term for any kind of vehicle, the sheriff's rig had been parked squarely in front of the donut shop. There was no way Lissa's husband, Sheriff Gage Christensen, wouldn't have sat with them. There was no way he wouldn't have asked Ryan how LA was treating him, and God knew what else. But the sheriff's truck had pulled out of its parking space just as they were pulling in, and Ryan had dodged yet another bullet.

After breakfast, he'd had the inspired idea to order sandwiches to go. A picnic at the actual waterfall that Rust Creek Falls had been named after had given him time alone with Kristen. He hadn't had to fear being unmasked at any moment by a friendly townsperson who might remember him from the flood cleanup. They'd seen no other humans on their afternoon hike. No grizzlies, either, and the placid but alarmingly large moose they'd spotted had been completely uninterested in meeting the new guy in town.

There'd been no dinner date.

Alone with his laptop was not how he'd hoped to end the night, but Kristen was at her mystery job in Kalispell. She'd given him one clue. Her job would help her become outrageously overqualified in the high school principal's eyes. Ryan had pretended not to guess the obvious, that she was teaching a night course.

He loved Kristen's determination. She'd win that teaching job sooner or later. Kristen as a cowgirl, home renovator and schoolteacher was an adorable combination. Kristen was perfect as she was, where she was. He couldn't ruin her life with his selfish desire to have her waiting for him in his beachfront high-rise at the end of his fourteen-hour days.

Sometimes the pursuit of happiness ended in a dead end.

It didn't have to end immediately, at least. Once she knew who he was and the limits of what he could offer, she might choose to be his long-distance lover. It couldn't last forever, but a few months of anticipating insanely heavenly weekends was as good as his life was going to get.

But if she said no when she found out how little he really had to offer her, he wouldn't be able to stop her walking away sooner rather than later.

One thing was inescapable: sooner or later, it was going to hurt like hell.

Chapter Eleven

"We never did go horseback riding yesterday. He wanted to go back out to the falls again. He thinks our falls are as pretty as Glacier National Park."

"Which you went to on Tuesday?"

"Right."

Kristen whispered the details of her week to her sister as they stood in the wings of the theater. Tonight was the final dress rehearsal, which meant she had to press down the hoop skirts of her blue Victorian gown to get close enough to her sister to whisper.

"And?" Kayla whispered. "Are you sleeping with him?"

"It was rated R, not X. But it was romantic, just the two of us." Kristen wriggled a little with the happiness of the memory. The motion added to her joy, because it was fun to make her skirt sway side to side.

"It's been just the two of you all the time. Awfully

private." Kayla was wearing regular clothes, all black from head to toe, the standard uniform of a stagehand. She had volunteered to serve as the prop master for half of the schedule.

"We don't always go off alone. You went to lunch with us today."

Ryan had driven her to Kalispell for buffalo burgers and sinful fries. It had been his suggestion to invite Kayla. Kristen had sworn Kayla to secrecy, though. She couldn't tell Ryan about tonight's dress rehearsal, only that she'd give Kristen a ride home after work.

"I want him all to myself. Kayla, I'm so happy when I'm with him. If he asked me to marry him today, I'd say yes."

"Silence on stage," the director called from his seat in the third row.

Kristen tried not to giggle like a disobedient child. She looked at Kayla, her partner in the crime of whispering, but Kayla was absentmindedly trailing her fingers over a bit of the black velvet trim on Kristen's gown, looking so sad that Kristen immediately felt sad, too. What had she said to put that look on her sister's face?

Marriage. It dawned on Kristen that she'd been taking giant steps since this summer, moving out, finding work, expanding her horizons. Most of all, falling in love. Maybe Kayla was feeling excluded.

Before Kristen could give her sister a squeeze and whisper that she shouldn't worry, that nothing could change the bond they shared as identical twins, Kayla yawned. She looked so tired. Come to think of it, she'd been sort of sad and tired for a while now, long before Ryan came back to town.

Without thinking further, Kristen put her hand on her sister's forehead.

"What are you doing?" Kayla whispered, jerking away in surprise.

"Do you feel okay? You seem kind of down."

"I'm fine."

"Maybe we should get you a chair."

"Really, I'm fine. I'm just a little…"

"A little what?"

Kayla squared her shoulders, and pulled Kristen deeper into the wings. "I'm worried about you. Everything seems pretty sudden with Ryan."

"I've known him for months."

"You've known *of* him for months, but you've really only known him for days. Are you sure you're in love with Ryan Roarke, or are you in love with the idea that this cowboy has come to town who fits your image of the perfect man?"

Suddenly, Kristen felt like she was the one who needed the chair. Hearing Kayla whisper doubts after she'd finally met Ryan was a horrible turn of events. She wanted her sister to say Ryan was wonderful. She wanted her sister to say that, having met him, she understood now why Kristen had kept such faith in him for all these months.

"Don't look like that," Kayla whispered. "I just want you to be sure you're paying attention to the real man, not the idea of being in love with a man. I don't want you to be hurt again."

Understanding dawned. "He's nothing like that stupid pilot. Ryan's like us. He worked with us in the stables twice this week. Didn't you think he loved all our twin stories over lunch today? He understands loyalty, and family, and—and love." But she hesitated over the last word, because Ryan hadn't said he loved her.

Really, she hadn't said she loved him, either. They hadn't talked about their future as a couple, only that he loved being with her and would come back as soon as he could. Maybe Kayla was right. Maybe she hadn't been paying enough attention to the real man.

The theater was plunged into darkness, her cue to take her place center stage before the lights went up on her big scene. It was time for Belle to make things perfectly clear with Ebenezer. Then she'd walk away and leave him alone in a spotlight as artificial snow began to fall.

Kristen picked up her fur muff and hurried to her mark. Belle needed to have a lot of courage to be so frank with Ebenezer about their relationship.

A little shiver ran down Kristen's back.

It's just a touch of stage fright.

But it wasn't. She couldn't stay in her happy fog much longer. She needed some of Belle's courage to ask Ryan exactly where their relationship stood. Tomorrow.

Kristen took her spot and waited for the curtain to rise. There was nothing to fear. She knew her part and she trusted her crew.

She had nothing to fear tomorrow, either. Ryan was no Ebenezer. Ryan would never place his career before her. In real life, she wouldn't be walking out of the spotlight and into his past.

"Oh, my gosh. It's my Mrs. Claus."

Kristen squeezed Ryan's hand in excitement, pulling him to a stop in front of the thrift shop. They'd had lunch in Kalispell again, and were window-shopping in the quaint part of town, the part that included Depot Park and the theater. Tonight was opening night. So thrilling—but so was finding Mrs. Claus.

"Do you think she's the right size? I don't think she's four feet. She might be the three-foot version. They made that in 1970. I've got the 1968 Santa. He's bigger."

"Maybe your Santa likes his women petite. I do."

Kristen bumped him with her shoulder, and he smiled his not-quite-a-smile.

Pay attention to the real man.

Her sister's words had been haunting Kristen all day. She looked at Ryan more closely as they stood outside the window. Its entire display was of Santas. Large ones, small ones, ugly atrocities from dime stores, all were mixed in with porcelain antiques. It was a dizzying array of red suits and white beards, but Ryan had already turned his back on it. That half smile said it all: he wasn't comfortable.

"Do dolls creep you out?" Kristen had gone to college with a girl who had a genuine phobia about dolls. To this day, Kristen felt bad about teasing her before she'd realized just how real the girl's aversion had been.

"Dolls?" Ryan looked at her with that brow raised in surprise. "Hardly. Did you want to watch a horror movie tonight or something?"

It was her turn to laugh uncomfortably. "No, I've got something else planned." His ticket to tonight's show was burning a hole in her pocket. She pointed at the store window, stretching the blue crochet of her mitten with her index finger. "So, it's Santa Claus, then. You don't care for Santa?"

He was about to say no, she knew it, but then he shook his head and looked at her like she was an unusual creature of some sort. "You really pick up on the strangest things. You're right. I don't care for Santa. I'm not a big fan of Christmas in general."

She remembered his words from the summer. "You said once if anyone could make Christmas better, it would be me."

"The decorations definitely look better when you're in front of them." His words were light and teasing, but Kristen knew she wasn't imagining the guarded look in his eyes.

"I thought you meant I'd make a good thing better, but you meant make a bad thing tolerable, didn't you?" She should have been paying attention. Tonight's play had scene after scene that included carolers and Christmas trees. "Just how averse are you to Christmas?"

Ryan turned to look at the street, with its red bells and green garland stretched between stores and giant candy canes tied to every pole. Then he looked back to the window full of Santas. "Most of this is fine. I hadn't really made the distinction, but you're right. It's Santa that particularly bothers me."

His attention was all on her. For once, it made her uncomfortable.

She tried for a nonchalant shrug.

"I don't believe in aggravating old injuries. You told me once about the church steps, and I think it's smart to just avoid them. There's a side entrance to the church, so why stand on the steps when you don't have to?"

Why go to a Christmas play when you don't have to?

She wouldn't give him the ticket. It was so disappointing, but really, she wouldn't make him do something unpleasant for the sake of her pride. She'd wanted him to see her onstage, but he'd love her just the same if he avoided a play that made him cringe.

He hasn't said he loves you. Pay attention.

Fine. Then he'd care for her just the same whether he saw her onstage or not.

She loved him, though, and she was concerned for his comfort. "Avoiding church steps or whatever else is unpleasant is simple enough, but avoiding Santa Claus... I don't think it's possible. December must be torture for you."

The sting of tears caught her by surprise. Disappointment, concern, love for a man who was leaving two days from now, her uncertain future—all of it added up. She puffed out a little breath and blinked back the tears quickly.

Not quickly enough. Ryan pulled her protectively into the alcove by the window. "Is that a showstopper? I didn't think that would make a woman consider walking away." The stiffness with which he asked the question was a sure sign that this was not a passing curiosity. This question mattered.

A woman walking away. Pay attention.

"What if you have children someday? Would you raise them without Santa?"

He was silent for an eternity.

She felt awful, keeping him by this window full of Santas. "We can keep walking. We don't even have to talk about this."

To her surprise, he enveloped her in a hug. "It's okay. I've never dated a woman who made me think about having children."

She hugged him back, grateful once more that he was leaving the rodeo forever. It sounded like a rotten life.

He let go of her and cleared his throat a little, a man prepared to make a formal statement. "I think children deserve to believe in the magic of it all."

Kristen let out the breath she'd been holding. If she'd had time to think up a right answer, that would have been it.

"I'd handle it." To her relief, Ryan winked at her. "You'll notice I'm standing in front of this window without going crazy at the moment. I didn't run screaming from the Santa on your porch. I'm a grown man, I can control my feelings. If I was with a child who wanted to sit in Santa's lap, I could stand in that line at the mall for as long as it took. Does that answer your question?"

She smiled and nodded and pretended she wasn't choked up by those tears once more. Poor Ryan. Her Ryan. The one she was paying attention to.

She started walking toward Depot Park and her theater. Ryan fell in step beside her, and she reached out to hold his hand, blue mitten to his black leather driving glove. Only one event in his childhood could have given him such an aversion to Christmas. "Did you see Santa before or after your birth mother walked away?"

He whistled softly. "Has anyone ever suggested the law to you as a career? You're so fearless in your questioning. I can just see you with a witness on the stand."

That surprised her, in a good way. She swung their hands a little bit. "I like that image. It makes me sound tough. Much more flattering than what my brothers would say. They say I'm like a bull in a china shop, always jumping in without thinking."

"No, it's an insightful question. Childhood memories are tricky, though."

"You were three, right? I'm trying to come up with a memory from when I was three. I don't think I have any."

"I was almost four, but I still only remember a couple of moments."

They'd come to an intersection with a traffic signal. Ryan pushed the button, and out of habit, Kristen shifted from foot to foot to stay warm while they waited for the signal to walk. She'd been doing that since she was a little girl.

"When I was three, my sister and I were taken to a preschool here in Kalispell once a week while my mother did the big shopping. I really only know that because my mom has pointed out the preschool to me and told me about it."

"The big shopping?"

"You know, the weekly grocery stock-up. My brothers went through boxes of cereal, so she bought them by the gross."

The light turned green, and they continued walking hand in hand, like grown-ups.

"Anyway, I suspect the preschool was a way for her to get her shopping done without hauling around two three-year-olds, but she insists that it was to improve our social skills. If you think about it, it would be easy for twins on a ranch to grow up without ever seeing other children their age. I don't remember the preschool at all, or at least I thought I didn't, but I remember this toy kitchen. It was made of wood, but it had a stove and sink, and the knobs were blue. I asked my mom once what happened to it, who had we given it away to, and she said we never had a toy kitchen. It had been at this preschool."

She slowed her steps, concentrating on that memory, and Ryan slowed down with her.

"That's it. I can't remember the classroom or any of the other kids or what the teacher looked like. I remember blue kitchen knobs. Isn't that weird?"

"I'm told that's normal. Below a certain age, you might remember something like the candles on a birthday cake, but you wouldn't remember the whole day, like who was at the party or what gifts you got. Just an image of a flaming cake."

"You were told that?"

"Part of the adoption process included counseling for my parents as well as me. I don't remember that, either, but to this day, my parents recommend it to other adopting parents. When I was old enough to ask questions, they always seemed to know what to expect. I asked about the church steps when I was in middle school. Before that, they weren't sure I had any memory of my birth mother at all."

His adoptive parents must have cared about their new son very much to have prepared themselves to answer all his questions in the future. She'd like to meet them some day.

"Is that all you remember? Church steps and the backs of her legs and the hem of her skirt?"

"It's like one of those six-second videos that you see on the internet. I'm looking down at my shoes, and I'm standing on cement steps. I know it's a church, and it's some kind of Christmas festival, because I'm holding a snow globe. It's brand-new to me, like I've just gotten this snow globe, and my shoes hurt, and my mother..."

He trailed off into silence.

"I'm sorry," Kristen said. "I shouldn't have asked you to relive that."

He looked almost surprised at her apology. "It's okay. I was just replaying that scene, and you were right. I would have said that Santa wasn't part of it, but he was. That snow globe had a little plastic Mr. and Mrs. Claus in it, puckered up for a kiss and bending toward each other with their eyes closed."

"Oh, no. Like the one on my porch?"

"It's a common scene. I dropped the snow globe when she walked away. There was water and glitter splattered everywhere, and those red figures were lying there in the open air, still straining toward each other, still trying to connect. They never get to kiss, do they?"

They reached the park, which was really just an open square. Soon, it would be filled with cocoa stands and craft stalls for the official start of the holiday season. Right now, in the sunny-cold afternoon, it was a still-green square by the railroad tracks, empty except for the plain evergreen in the center that awaited its holiday finery.

Kristen stopped walking and turned to face Ryan. "Why didn't you tell me? I would have retired Mr. Claus. I would have at least shut up about my quest for Mrs. Claus."

"Unnecessary, remember? I can handle it."

She felt the tears sting her eyes. "Right. Because you're a big, tough man and you can control your feelings."

"Is that so bad?"

She stepped into him, her boots fitting between his as she clutched his lapel in her mittens and looked up at him through lashes that were wet with tears. "I'm so very sorry. I'm sorry that Ryan Michaels had to learn to control feelings like those. And I'm sorry that Ryan Roarke has a girlfriend who is too curious. I shouldn't have been so nosy."

"Don't be sorry. I want you to know me." He lifted her chin with his leather-gloved hand and kissed away a tear. "You are so special because you want to know me. It's a gift to be with a woman who asks such real questions. Most women just want—"

He cut himself off abruptly.

"Women just want what?"

Long moments ticked by. At first, she was horrified that she'd brought up some other terrible memory, but when he wouldn't quite meet her gaze, she looked at him harder. What did women want from him?

"Oh, my gosh," she blurted. "You're blushing, aren't you?"

"Of course not."

"You are." She slapped the lapel of his overcoat with her palm. "That's what women want from you, huh? I guess I'm not very unique."

They both began to laugh, and it felt wonderful to be with him, laughing by an evergreen on a sunny day in the park.

"Kristen." Ryan pulled her to him. "You are the most perfect you. Never has a woman touched my heart the way you do."

Her heart soared at those words, and she looked up at him through lashes that were still dotted with tears. "With you, I'm crying one minute and laughing the next. I think that definitely means I love you."

"Are you sure you can love a man who is more of a Scrooge than a Santa?"

If only he knew. "Scrooge had his reasons for hating Christmas, and so do you. I'd have to have a heart of stone to hold it against either one of you. I've always had a soft spot for Scrooge."

"I've always liked Scrooge, too." His eyes narrowed the tiniest bit, and then he straightened and looked around the square. Red bells, candy canes, the tree awaiting its decorations—he looked critically at them all. "I've always thought I hated Christmas, but I don't. None of this bothers me. I watch at least one version of Scrooge every year."

"You do?" The ticket in her pocket might be a sweet surprise, after all.

"I do. I don't hate everything about Christmas."

"Just Santa?" she asked, wanting to be sure.

"Yeah, I'm not so crazy about him, but now I've pinpointed why. Thank you. I told you those questions were good ones."

"Being like Scrooge could be a good thing. He changes at the end of the play and ends up as the biggest Christmas fan of them all."

"That may be a bit ambitious, but I'll work on it."

"The day after Thanksgiving, there's a big parade through town that ends right here. The mayor lights the tree, and it stays lit all month. When you come back, I'm going to bring you here and kiss you until you have a great Christmas memory to start building on."

His smile dimmed a little at her words, but that was probably because a great Christmas was a new concept for him. "I told you when we met that if anyone could make Christmas better, it would be you."

She looped her arms around his neck. "And when I find my 1968 Mrs. Claus, I'm going to put her on the porch with her little mouth pushed right up to Santa's. It's too sad that they never make that connection. Mine are going to get to kiss all winter long."

He'd said her questions were like a gift to him, but she had something better to give: a promise. So while he was still chuckling, she spoke very seriously. "And, Ryan Roarke, whether it is Christmas or the Fourth of July or spring or autumn, I will never, ever walk away from you."

Kristen loved him.

Him, Ryan Roarke, who had once been Ryan Michaels, and who bore all the complications that came with his history. Miraculously, he'd come to Montana and found the one woman who had taken the time to get to know him inside and out, and she loved him.

They'd spent all week sharing their histories, their feelings, their desires. She knew nothing about the cars he owned or the clients he helped, but she knew his heart. She loved him, the real him, not an idealized image of a cowboy or a rodeo star. He could tell her about his law practice now, and it wouldn't change anything she loved about him, because she'd fallen in love without knowing about his Hollywood connections or his bank account. When he explained that he couldn't make it back in December, that there'd be no kiss by the town's tree, she'd be disappointed, but she'd still love him in January.

"Speaking of Scrooge," she said, "there's something you don't know about me. Close your eyes."

He closed them obediently. He heard the rustle of her bright red coat as she unbuttoned it. His own coat was unbuttoned despite the temperatures staying in the thirties. In only one week, his body had learned to tolerate the cold far better. If he lived in Montana, it would take no time to adjust.

"Now let me turn you so you're facing this way."

If only he could live in Montana. He couldn't let his parents down, but he needed to find a way to see Kristen more often. December was impossible, but perhaps he could fly Kristen to Los Angeles, if she could juggle her ranch, her renovations and her teaching job. She'd never want to live in LA, but she might find a visit interesting.

"Okay, open your eyes."

Kristen was beaming at him as she held a ticket in her mittened hand.

He took the ticket. "*A Christmas Carol*? We were just talking about it. You had this in your pocket the whole time?"

"I did, but I wasn't going to give it to you if it would make you sad. You have no idea how relieved I am to hear you say you like Scrooge. Tonight is opening night, right here at this theater." She gestured toward the sprawling brick building she'd turned him to face, a renovated train depot, by the looks of it.

She seemed overly excited about attending a local play, but he was game. "Great. We'll go. You've got the other ticket?"

"That's the surprise. You know that job I've been working at every day? This is where I've been."

His brain made a feeble effort to tie a teacher into the theater. She tutored children in the cast, perhaps. Dread started building, knotting his gut. He tried to connect a cowgirl to the theater, grasping at straws. Perhaps there were live animals in the play, and she wrangled them. But his heart knew what was coming, what came next.

What always came next, with every woman.

"After I met you, I knew that it was time to get serious about my passion, my career, my life. Everything. Because of you, I'm pursuing a little happiness here in this theater. I don't need a ticket, because I'll be onstage."

No. Don't say it, don't break it.

"I'm an actress!"

Good God. He staggered back a step. How could he have thought it would be any different with this woman?

He crumpled her ticket into his fist and shoved his hands in his pockets. "You knew. All along, you knew."

Her smile didn't falter, but the little wrinkle between her brows betrayed her concern at his reaction. She wasn't a good enough actress to hide her concern.

"I knew? Well, yes, I auditioned in October."

"An actress." He looked at her beloved face—yes, beloved, damn it—and felt like a fool.

"You knew I was an actress."

He couldn't speak he was so disgusted.

Her smile was completely gone now, as she so earnestly tried to make him believe this was a good thing. "You were the one who encouraged me to use my degree. You were the one who inspired me not to take no for an answer."

"From a principal. So you could teach."

"So I could create a drama club. I majored in theater, Ryan. I'd love to direct a play at the school. I love the theater."

"Of course you do."

She blinked at his mocking tone and even pulled that

trick with the tears again. He wanted to applaud her performance, shout *Brava!* for the way she'd so thoroughly performed her part this week, but he couldn't go that far. Not yet. Not while she looked like the innocent ranch girl of his dreams. Once she made it to Hollywood— and he had no doubt that a woman with her exquisite features could get noticed there—she'd be Botoxed for no reason, her lips augmented and her hair dyed blond, and then, when she didn't look so much like Kristen, he'd be able to harden his heart completely.

Right now, it hurt like hell.

"Well done, Kristen. Well played. A word of caution, though. You almost gave away your game at the beginning of the week. You accepted the fact that my name was Roarke too easily. You should have played it a little less cool that I was from California. You were supposed to think I was a rodeo star, remember? There are no cattle operations in LA."

"But… Bakersfield. Salinas." She sounded faint. Bewildered. Still beautiful.

He couldn't bear to look at her. For a week, he'd been denying himself the pleasure of her body, wanting her to know who he really was before he made love to her.

He had to laugh at his own naïveté. "I must've thrown you off by refusing to share your bed, but you compensated brilliantly. All those long talks, all that tender concern. It was a novelty to me, I admit. What were you hoping for, Kristen? Was I supposed to go to your little play tonight and be so besotted that I'd run to Scorsese and sing your praises? What are you earning at this theater, equity minimum? Did you think I'd negotiate a top contract for you?"

She'd deserve it. The way she was pressing her little mittens to her temples in confusion, the way her hair tangled with her polka-dot scarf and the November breeze pinkened her cheeks—oh, yeah. She was playing her role to perfection. He could get her top dollar.

"It backfired," he informed her coldly. "The sex would have been fine. No hard feelings. But to make me believe in love and family and goddamned Santa Claus? I just feel like a sucker. No one does favors for people who treat them like suckers."

Kristen held her palms out in a helpless gesture. The gentle shake of her head was just enough to make fat tears drop from her lashes to her cheeks.

"Who *are* you?" she whispered, the plea in her voice sounding so real his heart squeezed hard in his chest.

"Did you really think I was a cowboy? The rodeo star of your dreams? Please."

Finally, she dropped the innocent shock and moved on to something else, something angry. The stomp of her booted foot and the clenching of her fists were perfect touches. "Stop this. Stop. You're being hurtful, and I don't know why. You're from Los Angeles and you were never in the rodeo? What on earth do you do?"

"I'm an attorney." He crossed his arms over his chest, closing his jacket against the cold. "An attorney in the entertainment industry, and a damned successful one, as you well know."

"An attorney."

"A simple thing to search for on the internet. I honor my confidentiality agreements, but Hollywood studios do not, when they want to stir up publicity. My role in the Century Films controversy became common knowledge. How convenient for actresses who are ready to take their careers to the next level."

"I searched Ryan Michaels, the rodeo rider. You lied to me."

"I never claimed to be in the rodeo."

"But you knew I thought so. All week, you've been lying to me. You let me spill my heart out—oh! When I told you about that lying, cheating pilot, you should have told me you were just like him. Just toying with me while you were in town. Just playing a game until it was time to fly off to some other life."

And she hated him for it, judging by the look on her face. He steeled himself against the pain. Maggie had predicted it, but Maggie hadn't known that Kristen had been playing him for a fool all along. This was just an act.

Kristen took in a shuddering breath. "Were you lying from the beginning, even in the summer? Were you really considering moving to Rust Creek Falls? Did you care for me even a little?"

He'd be damned before he told Kristen any more about his feelings. She didn't need to know that his parents' need for him to take over the firm had ended his dream to move here, either. But as he looked into her blue eyes, wide with hurt and bright with tears, some piece of Ryan wanted to hold her and soothe her and reassure her.

He squelched the impulse. "I'm not the actor here, Kristen. You are."

Let her make of that what she wanted.

The cold air had dried the tears on her cheeks. "You shouldn't play with people's lives. You shouldn't have hurt mine. I only loved you."

Ryan hated himself for how badly he wished that were true.

"I think we've covered everything sufficiently," he said. "There's no need for a dramatic ending. You'll forgive me if I don't wish you luck in your acting career. Goodbye, Kristen."

She closed her eyes, a moment of misery, and started to turn away. But she only began the motion with her shoulders before she stopped herself and leveled her gaze on him once more. She said nothing, did nothing.

He raised one brow. "Go on. Your theater awaits. I've got nothing left to say."

"You're waiting for me to walk away. I made you a promise before I handed you that ticket. I told you I would never walk away from you. I'm standing right here, Ryan. If you want to leave me, if you want this to end, then you are going to have to be the one who walks. I won't do that to you. Not even now."

Now that you've broken everything.

Nothing good lasted forever. Finding out that Kristen's love had been a lie was really nothing more than he'd expected. Actresses were always ambitious, after all.

Ryan turned on his heel and began walking away. He shoved his hands in his coat pockets and felt the ticket. Without missing a step, he pulled the crumpled ticket from his pocket and dropped it onto the sidewalk.

I'm not this good of an actress.

Kristen could hardly hold herself together. Her hands were shaking as she tried to button the tight cuffs of her Victorian costume.

"Do you need help?" Kayla stopped to put down the bowl and spoon Scrooge would be using to eat his gruel.

In her shapeless black clothes, with her headset on her head, Kayla looked ready to make sure all the props made it onstage throughout the performance.

"Oh, Kayla. I'm so glad to see you. I had the most awful day with Ryan."

"Hold that thought. One second."

Kayla dashed off to one of the toilet stalls in the women's dressing area, cutting Kristen short just when she'd been about to spill all her misery.

She shouldn't give in to the misery, anyway. She should get through the show before she let her feelings out, because once she started crying, she was afraid she'd never stop.

She managed the buttons on her cuff, then the other cuff. Still, her sister stayed in the bathroom. Kayla hadn't been herself for weeks now, and Kristen was worried sick about her. She couldn't handle any more bad news, not on top of Ryan's betrayal.

Ryan. She couldn't stop thinking about him for a second. How could she have been so deceived? A Hollywood attorney, playing at being a cowboy. They'd never actually done any riding or training of the horses this week, she realized suddenly. That had been by design. *His* design.

But, dear God, the horses had loved him, and so had she.

He'd lied to her.

He'd left her.

She pressed her hand to her mouth, physically trying to hold her sobs in. She couldn't do this. She couldn't go out on that stage and say her heartbreaking lines while her heart was truly breaking.

"We've got a full house." The stage manager's voice came over the little speaker that was kept backstage. "Two minutes to curtain."

She was about to find out whether or not she could. The show must go on.

Chapter Twelve

Kristen's tears didn't wait for their cue.

From the wings, where she hovered anxiously near Kayla's prop station, she watched the first scenes of the play. The little boy playing the youngest version of Ebenezer was doing a good job. Too good for Kristen's state of mind.

The little boy had no one to love him, no place to spend the Christmas holiday. His classroom was barren. One by one, every other student left with a mother or father. The teacher gave him a book to read and threw one measly piece of coal into the stove, then walked out. Alone, rejected, unwanted, the boy huddled at his wood desk.

In the dark cocoon of the wings, Kristen's tears fell. If young Ebenezer had just dropped a snow globe on the floor...

Poor Ryan. He'd been even younger than this boy

when he'd been left alone in the world. Thank goodness he'd been adopted, but despite thirty years of being a Roarke, Ryan was still the little boy who'd learned to be so careful with his heart. Kristen had thought she could prove to him that her love was unbreakable, as solid and real as the love his adoptive parents had given him, but he wouldn't give her the chance.

Maybe a man who'd spent thirty years avoiding pain, a man who'd only very carefully chosen to return the love of those immediate family members who'd spent years loving him first, maybe that man would never change.

She would never know.

The tears started anew, and Kristen knew she would have to repair her stage makeup. Quickly. The Christmas party scene at the jovial Fezziwig home was about to begin.

While the stage was blacked out, the stagehands rushed antique toys onto the set, setting them under the tree. Kayla rolled a rocking horse onto the stage, then she zipped back to the wings with her arms full of schoolbooks from the classroom scene. She placed them in their assigned spot at her station, then she put her hand on her stomach and gave herself a pat.

Kristen's sobs hiccupped to an abrupt stop. That pat was the kind of thing a pregnant woman did to her growing belly.

Kayla was pregnant.

No. They were sisters. Twins. Kayla would never keep such a secret from her. She wasn't even dating anyone. But the months of fatigue, the nausea, even the decision to give up caffeine…

The lights onstage came up, bright white to make the

colorful party set pop. The audience applauded the set design before the first line of dialogue could be spoken, and Kristen watched her sister smile and take her hand away from her stomach to applaud, too. The white lights bounced off her black clothes, and Kristen wanted to cry all over again. Her sister had a definite baby bump. The first secret Kayla had ever kept from her was one of the most important ones of all.

It didn't seem possible that two people Kristen loved had so completely hidden their real selves from her. From Ryan's livelihood to Kayla's new life, Kristen had been oblivious to it all, a trusting, blind fool. Like the character of Belle, she only wanted to go back to the way things had been.

Belle was brave, though. When the man she loved changed, Belle faced the truth. In the face of Ryan's betrayal, Kristen had no choice but to do the same.

With a swirl of blue velvet, she hurried back to the makeup station, suddenly thankful for the chance to play Belle tonight. For the length of a few pages of script, Kristen would get to be brave.

And then, when the lights went out and the audience left, she would fall apart.

The Ghost of Christmas Past showed no mercy.

Old Scrooge wanted to enjoy the happiest memory of his life, but the figure in white and flame dragged him away as the curtain came down, obliterating the sight of Fezziwig's party and the lively dancing.

Ryan shifted his weight as he leaned against the very back wall of the theater. The happiest memory of his life was a dance, too. A waltz in the middle of an empty road. A sky lit by fireworks, a woman's voice humming the melody that guided them. Destiny.

The bitterness threatened to choke him. Her perfection had been an act, just as her performance tonight would be. Ryan had decided to buy a ticket at the last minute. He didn't bother taking his seat, because he'd be leaving soon. He only wanted to see Kristen onstage before he caught the last flight out. He needed to witness all her fake glory as an actress. When the happier memories swamped him, as they already had while he'd gone back to his hotel and packed, he wanted to be able to recall her on the stage, pursuing the career that she'd hoped he would boost.

The Ghost of Christmas Past pointed to the center of the dark stage. Scrooge begged her not to show him the inevitable, but of course he had to turn toward center stage, as well.

In contrast to the full set of the Christmas party, this scene opened on a simple park bench lit by a single spotlight. Standing in the center of the circle of light was Kristen, absolutely breathtaking in her winter velvet gown. Snow gently fell all around her.

Ryan heard a hiss of breath and realized it was his own. Kristen looked like a figurine in a snow globe. He'd come for a memory. He didn't want this one.

A young man in top hat and tails entered the circle of light. Kristen looked at Ebenezer with such longing, such regret, that Ryan was taken aback. With talent to match her looks, the sky would have been the limit if he'd wanted to launch her career.

Eventually the words of the play penetrated his thoughts. "Tell me truly, if you saw me today for the first time, would you make the effort to dance with me at Fezziwig's party?"

Yes. A waltz or a two-step, a wooden floor or asphalt, anything at all to feel her in his arms one more time.

"The man who loved me is only a memory. For his sake, I pray you will be happy upon your chosen path. You no longer want me to walk with you, no matter how much I wish it otherwise."

For God's sake, he couldn't stand here and listen to this. Either she was a world-class actress stuck in an obscure regional theater in a tiny town, or her heart was truly breaking as she spoke her lines. Either way, it was her misfortune. She was the one who'd been planning on using him. She'd said everything he wanted to hear in exchange for her shot at Hollywood.

Impatiently, Ryan picked up his coat and gloves and headed for the exit. The usher stopped him at the door. Ryan would have to wait until the end of the scene to open the door into the bright lobby. From the corner of his eye, he saw the hem of Kristen's long skirt as she walked out of the spotlight and was swallowed by the darkness.

"Go after her, you fool," Old Scrooge cried.

The usher held up his finger. One minute more.

Old Scrooge implored his younger self with an urgency born of grief. "Do you not see her caring heart? Lift your eyes from that cursed gold ring. Go after her! It's not too late for you."

But it was too late. The Ghost's flame was extinguished, the scene went dark, the audience erupted into applause and Ryan got the hell out of there.

An hour later, as he settled into his seat on the evening's only flight out of Kalispell, the voice of the pilot came over the speakers. "Ladies and gentleman, this is Captain Toomer speaking. Along with the rest of your Denver-based crew, we'd like to welcome you aboard Flight 89."

Ryan dropped his head back against the seat. A crew out of Denver. What were the odds? He could be leaving the woman who'd lied to him by taking a flight piloted by the man who'd cheated on her. Given destiny's warped timing, the odds were good.

The pilot who had *allegedly* cheated on her. Kristen could have invented the entire story to manipulate Ryan's emotions. That story had made her look good, really. She was the one who knew how to be faithful. She'd implied that the experience had negatively colored her opinion of men from big cities. Men like him.

Ryan lifted his head, a sudden jolt of adrenaline making him alert. She'd said she didn't like men from big cities. If her goal had been to attract Ryan, why would she say she avoided men like him? If her goal was to move to Los Angeles, why would she insist she didn't want to leave her hometown?

You fool...do you not see her caring heart?

It had been a trick. She'd used reverse psychology, saying she wanted the opposite of her goal to make herself seem all the more innocent. That had to have been it. She'd hidden her ambition, so he'd let down his guard. Ryan rested his head back once more, settling in for the first leg of his journey home.

You fool...

That had to be the explanation, because if it wasn't, then he'd just shattered something priceless.

* * *

"Another scotch, son?"

"Sure." Ryan turned with the decanter in his hand, ready to fill his father's glass.

His father had no glass. He merely stood on his own patio, his swimming pool sparkling in the sun beyond him, and slipped his hands into the pockets of his slacks.

"Ah. You meant, am I having another scotch?" Ryan tried not to sound too bitter as he laughed. Leave it to Dad to make his point so subtly. "Last I checked, I was over twenty-one, and I'm not driving anywhere."

Thanksgiving dinner was over at the Roarke home, but no one was leaving. Shane and a noticeably pregnant Gianna had flown in from Thunder Canyon, so they were spending the holiday weekend in one of the guest suites of their parents' home. Maggie and Jesse and baby Madeline had flown in from Rust Creek Falls and were staying for the weekend, too. Ryan was staying, as well, although he lived in the city. He wasn't going to leave this mini family reunion to spend the night alone in his exclusive, sterile penthouse. He didn't need more of his own company.

The sliding glass doors were open, and the sounds of football on TV spilled onto the patio. Sometime in the third quarter, the kitchen would be raided for a second piece of pumpkin pie or the first cold turkey sandwich of the weekend. Every year, he looked forward to that as much as he looked forward to the formal, hot dinner earlier in the day. This year, he'd also looked forward to finding relief from the loneliness that had been crippling him in the week since he'd left Kristen. Surely, surrounded by the family he trusted, Ryan's heart would be eased.

Instead, he was the seventh wheel. His parents, Christa and Gavin, were one couple. Shane and Gianna, another. Maggie and Jessie. That left Ryan feeling the absence of Kristen Dalton more acutely than ever. Thankfully, his father kept excellent scotch.

Shane joined them, carrying baby Madeline, practicing for his own impending fatherhood. "I can't get over the weather here. You forget how warm winter can be. It's already snowed at the resort. The ski bunnies are thrilled, but it means the main color we're going to see from now until Easter is white, white and more white."

"Go to one of the local high school's basketball games. There'll be lots of color."

Shane and his father both looked at him in surprise. Ryan shrugged, unwilling to explain where he'd gotten that advice.

Kristen's solution for a winter white-out had been so enthusiastic. Practical, too. Despite her secret agenda, he had to acknowledge that she really knew Rust Creek Falls inside and out. There'd been nothing fake about that tour. She'd had him seriously imagining himself trading in his penthouse for a luxury log home somewhere on the outskirts of town.

Which wouldn't have helped her get noticed in Hollywood.

Ryan stared into his scotch. Kristen must have known who he was that first day, of course. He'd been sitting with Maggie in the church during the wedding. Surely people knew Maggie was related to Shane Roarke, celebrity chef. It would have been a simple thing for Kristen to connect Roarkes with LA and show business.

Of course, she'd pretended not to know Maggie's maiden name later, but Kristen was a very good actress. She must have seen them together and realized that Ryan could be her chance to get out.

Then why had she invited him to come in? Had he moved to Rust Creek Falls, her plans would have been thwarted, yet that's exactly what she'd tried to get him to do.

The attorney side of him, which he'd once thought was his only side, picked another hole in his story. When, on that first day, could Kristen have seen him with Maggie? Kristen hadn't been at the church. Maggie hadn't been at the park.

Ryan set the scotch down, untouched.

"Are you in or not?" Shane asked, holding up a dollar bill.

"What?" Ryan couldn't think straight. His loneliness was rapidly morphing into a sick sort of dread. He may have screwed up. He may have made the biggest mistake of his life.

"Are you putting a dollar down on the Cowboys this year or not?"

"Sure." Ryan had been betting on the Dallas Cowboys to win the Thanksgiving football game since childhood, when losing a dollar had meant financial pain for the two brothers. "I don't have any cash on me. Spot me."

Shane sighed as if being asked for a dollar were a terrible imposition. "Here. Hold the baby."

Madeline let herself be handed from one uncle to the other without fussing. A series of mundane little family events followed. Shane took his wallet out of his back pocket as Maggie and Jesse joined them on the porch. When Maggie held her hands out for her daughter, Madeline stoutly refused the offer and clung to Ryan's neck.

There was laughter and Maggie pretended to be out-raged at Madeline's preference for her uncle. Through it all, Ryan managed to stay on his feet and act sane. Inside, he was losing his mind.

Everything that had happened at the wedding had been real. Kristen hadn't been lying on the Fourth of July.

Ryan walked away from his family, carrying Madeline around the edge of the kidney-shaped pool to a lounge chair. He sat and stretched his legs out on the cushions. Madeline stretched herself out on his chest.

Away from the noise of his family, Ryan called upon his analytical side. Even if Kristen had started flirting with him innocently in July, this month had been a different story. On that late flight out of Montana, Ryan had decided it was entirely too coincidental for Kristen to have run into Maggie at the movies. She must have arranged it. Then she'd pulled off a performance as a lovesick woman that had been realistic enough to fool his sister into calling him back to Rust Creek Falls. He'd already been on his way, but Kristen hadn't known that. She'd had to use Maggie to be sure he returned.

The baby fussed a little, burrowing herself into a more comfortable sprawl on his chest. He patted the baby's back absently and stared at the blue water of the pool as she fell asleep. In the bright light of day, the sce-nario that had made sense on a midnight flight was full of holes so big, it didn't take an attorney to find them.

There was no movie theater in Rust Creek Falls. Mov-ies were only shown on a certain Fridays in the gym. Most of the town turned out for the basketball games, Kristen had said, and he was sure that was true for the movies, as well. It was quite possible that Kristen and

Maggie had run into each other there without any nefarious plotting on Kristen's part. Ryan only knew a handful of people in town, yet he hadn't been able to take Kristen to a donut shop without running into Lissa's husband, the sheriff.

For the rest of his theory to work, Kristen had to have known not just that he was a Roarke, but that Maggie Crawford was, too. The biggest proof of Kristen's innocence was her sister. Kayla was Kristen's twin, her confidante, her biggest cheerleader. If Kristen had hatched a plan to hitch herself to Ryan for a Hollywood career, her twin would have known about it. Instead, when she'd learned that his last name was Roarke, her surprise had been genuine. *Are you related to Lissa Roarke, then?* Kayla was no actress. She and Kristen hadn't known he was a Roarke until he'd told them in the barn.

Case dismissed. Kristen was innocent, and he was a fool.

He'd shattered a snow globe once again. A thousand flakes of glitter and a hundred drops of water couldn't be put back together. Once upon a time, Christa Roarke had come and replaced the birth mother he'd lost. This time, no woman could replace Kristen Dalton. She was the only one he wanted. The only one he'd ever want.

Baby Madeline snuggled her soft head under his chin. Even a bachelor like Ryan knew that sleeping babies should not be messed with. His infant niece had him pinned to the chair when he wanted to pace restlessly. He wanted to hit a punching bag until he was too tired to think, but there'd be no escaping today. Ryan closed his eyes, remembering Kristen as he'd seen her last, a vision in Victorian blue, standing in a snow globe of a spotlight.

He had to try to fix this. He couldn't live the rest of his life alone like a bitter old Scrooge, angry at himself for not going after the woman with the caring heart. If putting a snow globe back together was impossible, then...

Then he'd be grateful that people weren't snow globes. He was going to fix this.

The baby wriggled. Ryan spread his hand across her back to calm her. Holding a baby, he realized, was even more soothing than brushing a horse. If he could win Kristen back, he'd give her all the horses she wanted, and as many babies as she desired.

Having babies meant getting married. It meant living together in one house as one family. He couldn't commute from Montana to LA and be a good husband and father. Ryan knew, without a doubt, that he'd want to raise his family in Rust Creek Falls, if he could find a way to make it happen. Unfortunately, he was a lawyer, not a cowboy, and there was barely enough legal work in Rust Creek Falls to keep Maggie busy four days a week.

Kalispell wasn't too far, and the town was easily four times the size of Rust Creek Falls. If he practiced law there, he'd never make as much money as he did here in LA, but he could make a good living. If he could win Kristen back, if he could fix the damage he'd caused, then he would never have to get on a plane and leave her behind again.

There was one thing he couldn't do if he moved to Montana. He couldn't run his parents' firm for them.

The sense of obligation was familiar. He wanted his parents to be happy. He wanted to help them out any way he could, but when any way meant he couldn't have a life with Kristen…

This was the point where he always got stuck, the point where he would give up and do something mind-numbingly physical. Not today. The baby breathed evenly, her little rib cage expanding gently under his hand, forcing him to stay still. Forcing him to find a solution.

He didn't have one.

The sound of his mother's laughter carried over the pool water. Ryan opened his eyes and took in the scene. Parents, siblings, their spouses. More babies on the way. His family. His foundation.

He didn't have a solution, but he did have a family. He hadn't trusted Kristen's love—a crucial mistake. But in many ways he hadn't trusted in his family's love, either. He'd once told Kristen that he knew his parents wanted him to be as happy as Shane and Maggie, but he'd been afraid to put it to the test.

It was time he stopped silently taking on problems alone. Tonight, over pumpkin pie and turkey sandwiches, he'd rely on the family he trusted to decide the future of Roarke and Associates together.

Then he'd get on the first plane back to Montana. Would a permanent move to Rust Creek Falls be enough to convince Kristen to give him a second chance? He'd shattered that snow globe in such a spectacularly awful way that he wanted something equally spectacular to prove he'd never lose his faith in her again. He needed some way to demonstrate that he would never again be the cold-hearted bastard he'd been when he'd left her.

Madeline's tiny fist gripped his shirt as she slept. He kissed the top of her head. Kristen's words came back to him. *What if you have children someday? Would you raise them without Santa?*

Ryan ran the tip of his finger over the dimples in the back of Madeline's hand. "You deserve a chance to believe in the magic, little one. For you, I could tolerate Santa."

The germ of an idea started to form.

Carefully, he got to his feet and carried his niece over to the family. "Maggie. Shane. I need your help. Who do you know in the mayor's office in Kalispell?"

Chapter Thirteen

There was no performance on the day after Thanksgiving.

Kristen should have been thankful for the respite. Tonight, she wouldn't have to relive the horrible feeling of losing the man she loved. Instead, she had to play a role that seemed even more daunting. She had to ride on a float in a Christmas parade, smiling and waving and throwing candy and generally acting like she was in a happy holiday mood.

The entire cast of *A Christmas Carol* was assembled on a flatbed truck that had been turned into a float. Kristen wore her full costume. In addition to the corset and hoops, the heavy skirt and tight bodice, she carried a faux fur muff and wore modern long johns under her dress, because tonight, the snowfall was real.

They waited at one end of Main Street near a high school band, a motorcycle club and a cluster of rodeo riders whose horses were dressed to the nines in silver saddles and fancy tack. Kristen looked away from the rodeo riders.

The last float featured Santa Claus himself, who would join the mayor in lighting the Christmas tree in Depot Park.

Santa Claus. The symbol of everything magical and wonderful about the holidays for her was a symbol of misery for Ryan. Was it any wonder that a man who didn't believe in Santa couldn't believe that her love was real, either?

It took every bit of acting skill she had to look happy through the entire parade. Two miles had never crawled by so slowly, but her ordeal wasn't over yet. Because of their picturesque costumes, the cast had been asked to wait by the Christmas tree until Santa's float arrived. When Santa lit the tree, the cast would add charm and holiday spirit to the town's official photos. They would be posted on websites and spread around social media. The exposure would have been nice if Kristen was trying to get jobs outside her hometown, but no matter what Ryan Roarke thought, she wasn't. The only things she'd get out of this photo session were frozen toes.

She stamped her feet and clutched her hands more tightly together inside her muff. The cast had been on the first float. Santa was on the last.

"Okay, let's have everyone line up now, half on each side of the tree." The Kalispell newspaper photographer also doubled as the wedding photographer for most of the couples in town, so he was pretty quick about getting everyone posed, ready and waiting.

Hurry, Santa. I want to go home. It's been at least five hours since I last cried. I'm overdue.

At last, the float with Santa's cardboard and plywood sleigh arrived. Kristen plastered on her smile when the cameras started to flash.

Santa dismounted his float with ease, moving in a way that was far more sprightly than his white beard would indicate he was capable of. This year's Santa was as tall as he was wide. He worked his way through the crowd, passing out candy canes to the children, who jumped excitedly at the sight of him. With every "ho, ho, ho," the children squealed in delight. Kristen's stiff smile relaxed into something more genuine, as well.

"Ho, ho, ho. Merry Christmas."

Kristen jerked her gaze away from the children to study Santa instead.

"Merry Christmas," Santa called again.

He sounded like Ryan.

Her mind was playing tricks on her. Ryan was in LA, where he belonged. Her sister had made some polite small talk with Lissa Christensen the day after Kristen and Ryan's fight, and Lissa had said that her cousin had left a day early, probably to put out a fire at his law firm.

Kristen knew he'd only wanted to get away from her as quickly as he could. He'd been so full of self-righteous anger—all of it directed so unfairly at her—that he'd wanted to put a thousand miles between them.

Kayla had also broken the mortifying news to her that if Lissa was Ryan's cousin, that meant Maggie Crawford was Ryan's sister. Apparently, she was Maggie *Roarke* Crawford. When Kristen remembered that meltdown at the movies, she didn't know how she'd ever look Maggie in the eye again.

"Smile, please. Keep smiling." The photographer

hadn't stopped snapping yet. Kristen obediently forced her face into a semblance of happiness.

"Ho, ho, ho."

Honestly, that man sounded just like Ryan. Impossible—even if Ryan had returned to town to visit his sister or cousin, he would never, ever be caught dead in a Santa suit.

With his sack of candy canes now empty, Santa walked to the tree and shook the mayor's hand. The switch was thrown, the lights came to life and the crowd went wild. So did the camera flashes.

Santa chose to stand right between the only two women, Kristen and the actress playing Mrs. Cratchit. It could have been Kristen's imagination, but Santa seemed to give her an extra warm squeeze. Was Mrs. Cratchit feeling such a strong arm around her waist?

"Ryan…?"

This man didn't seem to be angry at her at all. Considering how furious Ryan had been just days ago, it couldn't be him. Then again, Santa was an important role. Santa could never get angry in front of children—and Ryan would never ruin Christmas for a child, despite its having been ruined for him.

But Ryan also had no earthly reason to ever wear a Santa suit. Whoever this year's Santa was, it couldn't be the man who'd so recently broken her heart. It was pitiful that she missed Ryan badly enough to imagine it was him.

At last, the ceremony was over, the photographer was satisfied, and the cast was free to return to the theater to remove their costumes. Santa offered Kristen his arm as she headed across the green to the theater, and they each smiled and returned waves from the children and adults they passed.

They entered the theater through the stage door, which led almost directly to the black curtains of the wings. Santa looked all around, turning in a full three-sixty. "Are there any children here? No? Good. I'd hate to confuse the little kids."

He pulled off his hat with one hand and his white beard with the other, and turned to kiss Kristen, hard.

She hadn't seen his face, but it didn't matter. She recognized his kiss.

"Ryan." She murmured his name against his lips, but before she could begin to ask him the questions his presence raised, he spoke.

"I'm so sorry. Please forgive me for being a stubborn, pigheaded jerk."

"But…" She shook her head at his padded costume, just one more mystifying piece of the puzzle that was Ryan. "Why?"

"Because I hurt you. I jumped to all the wrong conclusions, and I refused to listen to you when you told me the truth. I don't deserve it, but please forgive me."

"I meant, why are you Santa Claus? This is like your worst nightmare."

"Not even close. Losing you is my worst nightmare."

Most of the actors had made their way back to the dressing rooms, but Ryan pulled her deeper into the wings, where the black curtains muffled their voices and gave them a sense of privacy.

"I'm wearing this suit so you'll know that I mean it when I promise you that I won't make the same mistakes twice."

"You won't assume I'm some kind of gold-digging, movie star wannabe?"

Well, that had rolled off her tongue a little too easily. She'd had a week to relive every painful word he'd said to her, though.

He dropped his head for a moment, chagrined, then looked at her again with such tenderness in his expression, it took her breath away. "For starters, yes. That kind of mistake. I'm so sorry. Do you know why I assumed the worst? Because those were the only type of women I'd known. They were the only type of women I dated, because they couldn't hurt me. They didn't matter. If they walked away, nothing inside me would shatter."

He touched her face with one hand, tentatively cupping her cheek, then stroking his thumb over her cheekbone. "But you, Kristen, you matter."

"Oh, Ryan." Kristen turned her face into his hand.

"I didn't know how to handle that. You are this wonderful, remarkable, beautiful woman who somehow fell into my hands, but I didn't know how to hold you. I was so afraid I'd lose something good, that I was paralyzed. I did nothing. That was a mistake, too.

"I was afraid to lie to you and afraid to tell you the truth at the same time. I told myself you couldn't handle too many corrections all at once, but the only real truth was that I was petrified I'd lose the best thing in my life. That's you. That will always be you.

"I learned when I was young that nothing good lasts forever, but I don't think that's true any longer, not after meeting you. I believe forever is possible, a good forever, as long as I can spend it with you. I'm wearing this Santa suit because I'm not going to avoid the good things in life anymore. I hope that, someday, you'll love me again. I hope that you'll trust me not to make the same mistakes again."

Kristen swallowed past the lump in her throat. Just seeing his face again, just being touched by him again, made her happier than she could have believed possible just a short time ago. She pressed her hand to heart, feeling out of breath from the emotions.

"If you can't forgive me tonight, I understand," Ryan said. "I screwed up badly, but I'll be here tomorrow. And next week. Next year. You promised me you'd never walk away from me, and I'm here to make the same promise back. I'm staying. Right here in Montana, right here with you, until you believe me when I say I love you."

"Oh, Ryan." Kristen tried to throw her arms around his neck, but his red suit's padding was completely in the way. Her hoops pushed gracefully behind her when she got close to him, but his stuffed belly stayed stuffed.

Ryan unbuttoned the coat and tossed it on a folding chair. Underneath, he was wearing a fitted black T-shirt with the baggy red velvet pants. He pulled her into his arms and held her against his strong chest almost as tightly as she'd dreamed for the past lonely week.

"I don't want you to settle for a Scrooge when you want a Santa," Ryan whispered. "I don't want you to settle for a lawyer when you want a cowboy."

"I don't want a lawyer or a cowboy. I want a Ryan."

"Michaels or Roarke?"

"Both, as long as he's happy with me."

"He couldn't be anything else with you in his life, and that's the whole truth."

Kristen kissed him almost as passionately as she knew she'd be kissing him tonight. In her house. Finally.

The cast of the play had begun filtering back out of the dressing rooms. A man in street clothes whistled at their embrace. Kristen tried to brazen it out, giving the crew a nonchalant shrug of one shoulder as she broke off the kiss she'd initiated. She smoothed her gown into place over her hoops.

"Some things go without saying, but this needs to be said. I love you, Kristen Dalton. It's been seven days since I've held you, and I never want to go seven days without holding you again."

Ryan dropped to one knee in front of her, and Kristen thought her heart stopped. Cast, crew, costume—all were forgotten as she focused on Ryan.

He patted his oversize pants pockets and got a little of that deer-in-the-headlights look, but then he slid on his knee to the discarded Santa coat and dug through it until he came up with a gray velvet box. The theater people gathered around them began to buzz with excitement.

"I wanted to wear the Santa suit to show you how precious you are to me." He opened the gray box and held it up. The diamond ring inside sparkled with every color of every Christmas light ever strung on a cozy house for two. "This is the other way I want to show you how precious you are to me. I love you with all my heart, Kristen Dalton. I will never deserve you, but I'm not going to let that stop me from being happy with you. Will you marry me?"

The photographer by the town Christmas tree was tireless in his effort to capture the happiness of the newly engaged couple.

Kristen had changed into her street clothes, including a chic white jacket with faux-fur trim and the most flattering nipped-in waist. She'd bought it this week in a futile attempt to use retail therapy to soothe her heartbreak, but now she was thrilled to have something fabulous to wear for her engagement photos. Ryan was looking handsome and sexy and cute all at once. That was possible when the fine tailoring of a man's coat contrasted with the bright red Santa's hat he wore.

"Wassail!" One of the street vendors came up to their little cluster of friends and family. "It's on the house. Wassail to toast the happy couple."

Kayla was standing next to Kristen, so Kristen took the chance to offer her some sisterly advice. As surreptitiously as she could, she gestured toward her sister's thickening middle. "If I were you, I'd pass on the mystery punch this time."

Kayla colored. "I don't know what you mean."

"I know your secret. I want you to be as happy as I am. We've got to talk."

"Soon. Don't worry about me right now. This is your special night."

On Kristen's other side, Ryan scrutinized the two cups he held. "Do you suppose this is safe to drink? They still haven't solved the case of the Power of the Punch."

"I was just saying the same thing to Kayla. You and I have so much in common."

"On the other hand, we just got engaged. Who cares if the wassail is a little too strong?" He grinned at her, looking more carefree than she'd ever seen him look.

"It is a very old Christmas tradition." She took one of the cups from him.

"You know, Christmas is rapidly becoming my favorite time of the year. If I'm going to be a changed man like Scrooge, I believe I need to fully support all the traditions."

Kristen tapped her cup to his. "In that case, down the hatch."

"In that case, Merry Christmas to the future Mrs. Roarke." They drank to their own happiness, and kissed under the lights of the tree.

"From now on," Kristen sighed, "I'm always going to love wassail-flavored kisses."

"From now on," Ryan said, "I'm always going to love you."

* * * * *

*Don't miss the next installment of the new
Harlequin Special Edition continuity*

MONTANA MAVERICKS:
WHAT HAPPENED AT THE WEDDING?

*No one would ever guess that shy Kayla Dalton
is the writer behind popular gossip column
Rust Creek Ramblings. They'd be even more
surprised to learn she had a one-night fling with
Trey Strickland on the Fourth of July—and
he's about to get the Christmas gift of his life!*

*Look for
MERRY CHRISTMAS, BABY MAVERICK!
by Brenda Harlen*

*On sale December 2015, wherever
Harlequin books and ebooks are sold.*

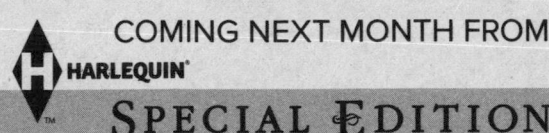

COMING NEXT MONTH FROM

HARLEQUIN®

SPECIAL EDITION

Available November 17, 2015

#2443 A COLD CREEK CHRISTMAS STORY
Cowboys of Cold Creek • by RaeAnne Thayne
When librarian Celeste Nichols's children's book becomes a success, she's stunned. Enter Flynn Delaney, her childhood crush, and his young daughter, who could use some of Celeste's storytelling magic since her mother passed away. With the help of Cupid and Santa, this trio might just have the best Christmas yet!

#2444 CARTER BRAVO'S CHRISTMAS BRIDE
The Bravos of Justice Creek • by Christine Rimmer
Carter Bravo wants to settle down...but he's not looking for love. So he asks his best friend, Paige Kettleman, to be his fiancée on a trial basis. What could go wrong? Neither Carter nor Paige can imagine that unexpected love is Santa's gift to them this year!

#2445 MERRY CHRISTMAS, BABY MAVERICK!
Montana Mavericks: What Happened at the Wedding?
by Brenda Harlen
Rust Creek Falls' top secret gossip columnist, Kayla Dalton, has the inside scoop on her high school crush, Trey Strickland. The Thunder Canyon cowboy is going to be a daddy! How does she know? Because she's pregnant with his baby!

#2446 A PRINCESS UNDER THE MISTLETOE
Royal Babies • by Leanne Banks
To protect herself, Princess Sasha Tarisse goes incognito as a nanny to handsome widower Gavin Sinclair's two young children. But what happens when the damsel-in-disguise and the dashing dad fall for one another under the mistletoe?

#2447 CHRISTMAS ON THE SILVER HORN RANCH
Men of the West • by Stella Bagwell
Injured rancher Bowie Calhoun claims he doesn't need a nurse, but he changes his mind when he sees gorgeous Ava Archer. Despite the sparks flying, the beautiful widow tries to keep her distance from the reckless playboy: she wants a family, not a fling! But not even Ava can resist the pull of true love...

#2448 HIGH COUNTRY CHRISTMAS
The Brands of Montana • by Joanna Sims
Cowboy Tyler Brand lives a carefree life—so he's shocked when his fling with London Davenport produces a baby-to-be. The Montana man is determined to do right by London, but she's got secrets aplenty to keep them apart. It'll take a Christmas miracle to get these two together forever!

YOU CAN FIND MORE INFORMATION ON UPCOMING HARLEQUIN® TITLES, FREE EXCERPTS AND MORE AT WWW.HARLEQUIN.COM.

Quiet librarian Celeste Nichols doesn't expect the success of her children's book. But even more surprising is the family she finds under the mistletoe this year with childhood crush Flynn Delaney and his daughter!

Read on for a sneak preview of
A COLD CREEK CHRISTMAS STORY, the latest book in RaeAnne Thayne's fan-favorite series,
THE COWBOYS OF COLD CREEK.

"Okay," Olivia said in a dejected voice. "Thank you for bringing me down here to meet Sparkle and play with the puppies."

"You are very welcome," Celeste said. "Any time you want to come back, we would love to have you. Sparkle would, too."

Olivia seemed heartened by that as she headed for the reindeer's stall one last time.

"Bye, Sparkle. Bye!"

The reindeer nodded his head two or three times as if he were bowing, which made the girl giggle.

Celeste led the way out of the barn. Another inch of snow had fallen during the short time they had been inside, and they walked in silence to where Flynn's SUV was parked in front of the house.

She wrapped her coat around herself while Flynn helped his daughter into the backseat. Once Olivia was settled, he closed the door and turned to Celeste.

"Please tell your family thank-you for inviting me to dinner. I enjoyed it very much."

"I will. Good night."

With a wave, he hopped into his SUV and backed out of the driveway.

She watched them for just a moment, snow settling on her hair and her cheeks while she tried to ignore that little ache in her heart.

She could do this. She was tougher than she sometimes gave herself credit. Yes, she might already care about Olivia and be right on the brink of falling hard for her father. That didn't mean she had to lean forward and leave solid ground.

She would simply have to keep herself centered, focused on her family and her friends, her work and her writing and the holidays. She would do her best to keep him at arm's length. It was the only smart choice if she wanted to emerge unscathed after this holiday season.

Soon they would be gone, and her life would return to the comfortable routine she had created for herself.

As she walked into the house, she tried not to think about how unappealing she suddenly found that idea.

Don't miss
A COLD CREEK CHRISTMAS STORY by
New York Times *bestselling author RaeAnne Thayne,*
available December 2015 wherever
Harlequin® Special Edition books
and ebooks are sold.

www.Harlequin.com

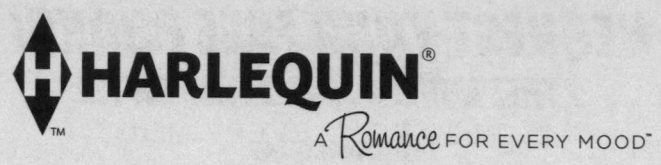

Love the Harlequin book you just read?

Your opinion matters.

Review this book on your favorite book site, review site, blog or your own social media properties and share your opinion with other readers!